One
The Cuckoo's Nest

A PLAY IN TWO ACTS

by *Dale Wasserman*

from the Novel by Ken Kesey

SAMUEL FRENCH, INC.

45 West 25th Street NEW YORK 10010
7623 Sunset Boulevard HOLLYWOOD 90046
LONDON *TORONTO*

ISBN 0 573 61343 5 Printed in U.S.A.

The *revised version of **ONE FLEW OVER THE CUCKOO'S NEST** published here opened Off-Broadway at the Mercer-Hansberry Theatre on March 23, 1971. It closed two and a half years later on September 16, 1973, after 1025 performances.

"Like a cartoon world, where the figures are flat and outlined in black, jerking through some kind of goofy story that might be real funny if it weren't for the cartoon figures being real guys..."

—One Flew Over The Cuckoo's Nest

SANKOWICH/GOLYN PRODUCTIONS

presents

DALE WASSERMAN S ONE FLEW OVER THE CUCKOO S NEST.

FROM THE NOVEL BY KEN KESEY

Production Designed by **NEIL PETER JAMPOLIS**
Produced by **RUDI GOLYN**
Directed by **LEE D. SANKOWICH**

CAST (In order of appearance)

Chief Bromden.. WILLIAM BURNS
Aide Williams...................................... WILLIAM PATERSON, JR.
Aide Washington................................ JOHN HENRY REDWOOD
Nurse Ratched .... JANET WARD
Nurse Flinn... EVE PACKER
Dale Harding .... JAMES J. SLOYAN
Billy Bibbitt ....LAWRIE DRISCOLL
Charles Atkins Cheswick III ....WILLIAM DUFF-GRIFFIN
Frank Scanlon.. JON RICHARDS
Anthony Martini ....DANNY DE VITO
Ruckly.. JOSEPH NAPOLI
Randle Partick McMurphy ....WILLIAM DEVANE
Dr. Spivey.. JACK AARON
Aide Turkel ....JEFFREY MILLER
Candy ....LOUIE PIDAY
Technician ....KELLY MONAGHAN
Sandy ....SYDNEYANDREANI
Voices....................................JOHN GARBER, DOUG ARMAND,
JOSEPH NAPOLI, DANNY RICH, MARC NELSEN, TEDDI KERN,
JAMES BARNETT, JOHN BLAKELEY, LEE D. SANKOWICH

*Following the Broadway production (credits on page 4), ONE FLEW OVER THE CUCKOO'S NEST was revised into two acts instead of the original three and rewritten to be performed by a smaller cast.

ONE FLEW OVER THE CUCKOO'S NEST by Dale Wasserman, based on the novel by Ken Kesey. Produced by David Merrick and Edward Lewis, in association with Seven Arts and Eric Productions, at the Cort Theatre, November 13, 1963.

CAST

(In Order of Appearance)

CHIEF BROMIEN .... *Ed Ames*
AIDE WARREN .... *Lincoln Kilpatrick*
AIDE WILLIAMS .... *Leonard Parker*
NURSE RATCHED .... *Joan Tetzel*
NURSE FLINN .... *Astrid Wilsrud*
DALE HARDING .... *William Daniels*
ELLIS .... *Arnold Soboloff*
BILLY BIBBIT .... *Gene Wilder*
SCANLON .... *Malcolm Atterbury*
CHESWICK .... *Gerald S. O'Loughlin*
MARTINI .... *Al Nesor*
RUCKLY .... *William Gleason*
FREDERICKS .... *Wesley Gale*
SEFELT .... *Charles Tyner*
COL. MATTERSON .... *Paul Huber*
RANDLE P. MCMURPHY .... *Kirk Douglas*
DR. SPIVEY .... *Rex Robbins*
AIDE TURKLE .... *Milton J. Williams*
CANDY STARR .... *Arlene Golonka*
NURSE NAKAMURA .... *Michi Kobi*
TECHNICIAN .... *Clifford Cothren*
SANDRA .... *K.C. Townsend*
AIDE .... *Peter Gumeny*

IMPORTANT BILLING AND CREDIT REQUIREMENTS

All producers of ONE FLEW OVER THE CUCKOO'S NEST *must* give credit to the Author of the Play in all programs distributed in connection with performances of the Play and in all instances in which the title of the Play appears for purposes of advertising, publicizing or otherwise exploiting the Play and/or a production. The name of the Author *must* also appear on a separate line, on which no other name appears, immediately following the title, and must appear in size of typ not less than fifty percent the sixe of the title type, substantially as follows:

(Name of Producer)
presents
ONE FLEW OVER THE CUCKOO'S NEST
by Dale Wasserman (50%)
Based on the novel by Ken Kesey (35%)

One Flew Over The Cuckoo's Nest

ACT ONE

SCENE: *The Day Room in a ward of a State Mental Hospital somewhere in the Pacific Northwest. A spacious, clean-lined expanse, impersonal and rather sterile. The furniture is plastic-covered. The trappings are at a minimum and disciplined in disposal. There are large, high windows opening on the ground level of a green world outdoors. Formidable locked steel grilles cover these windows, which are customarily left open. A door opens into the latrine. Next to this, a broom closet. There is a bulletin board, a magazine rack, a games cabinet and, on a pedestal, the patients' Log Book. A locked door leads to the hallway; another door, unlocked, to the dormitory. The Nurses' Station is a large booth, somewhat elevated. It has sliding glass panels through which the* CHARGE NURSE *may keep all the room under scrutiny. It is always kept locked. Through the glass may be seen drug cabinets set in the wall.* NURSES *sit at a desk facing the room; on this desk a telephone and a microphone, and to one side a tape recorder. These latter two feed into speakers set in the walls or ceiling of the Day Room. Mounted on the wall behind the desk there is an array of switches, dials, toggles and knobs through which the* NURSES, *with godlike power, can monitor lights, sound, TV, etc. At the foot of the Station there is a gray steel oblong, perhaps three feet long. This is the "panel" which houses the transformers, relays and electrical cables feeding into the Station. It has a squat, brutish look, disguised by cushions which allow it to be used as a bench. There is a TV set, kept against a wall when not in use. The arrangement of tables and chairs is flexible.*

AT RISE: *The stage is dark but for a single shaft of light on* CHIEF BROMDEN. *He is a huge, bull-muscled Indian who stands six and a half feet but when people are about carries himself like a small man. Head cocked, he is listening. He hears it: a whistling sound, soft and malignant; and vague and milky light-patterns wreathe and intertwine across the stage.*

CHIEF BROMDEN. (*Voice on tape.*) Papa? They're foggin' it in again. Somethin' bad is gonna happen, so they're foggin' it in. (*Moves, then pauses as there comes the soft, puissant thunder of machinery and, contrapuntally, the pinging rhythm of electronic music. Behind the glass of the darkened Nurses' Station colored lights pulse and dance accompaniment.*) There! You hear it, Papa? The Black Machine. They got it goin', eighteen stories down below the ground. They're puttin' people in one end and out comes what they want. The way they do it, Papa, each night they tip the world on its side and everybody loose goes rattlin' to the bottom. Then they hook 'em by the heels, and they hang 'em up and cut 'em open. Only by that time they got no innards, just some beat-up gears and things, and all they bleed is rust. You think I'm ravin' 'cause it sounds too awful to be true, but, my *God*, there's such a lot of things that's true even if they never really happen!

(*A BELL RINGS. The sounds and dancing lights are gone, and the STAGE LIGHTS UP with the effect almost of an explosion. Whistling is heard from off as the* AIDES *approach.* CHIEF BROMDEN *freezes into the catatonic stance. A key hits the lock, and* AIDES WARREN *and* WILLIAMS *enter, their rubber-soled shoes making no sound. They wear starched and spotless white uniforms and they lope in tandem or abreast like a team of splendid, lithe panthers.*)

WARREN. Well, well, here's the Chief.

WILLIAMS. The soopah-Chief.

WARREN. Ol' deef an' dumb.

WILLIAMS. Had his breakfas' an' rarin' to go.

WARREN. (*Coming close to* CHIEF BROMDEN.) Don' you know better? Don' you know keep to your room till that bell ring? (CHIEF BROMDEN *slides away.*) Haw, look at 'im shag it! Big enough t'eat apples off my head and he scared like a baby!

WILLIAMS. What you want, baby? Yo' broom? (*Going to fetch it.*) Thassit. He want his broom.

WARREN. Ol' Chief Broom. Thassit, baby, thassa good loony.

WILLIAMS. (*Thrusts the broom into* CHIEF BROMDEN'S *hands.*) Start sweepin', baby.

WARREN. Ol' Broom Bromden.

WILLIAMS. Ol' Chief Broom.

(*They bray with laughter. Unseen by them* NURSE RATCHED *has entered. She is a handsome woman, perhaps in her forties . . . hard to tell. There is an odd perfection about her: face smooth as flesh-colored enamel, skin a blend of white and cream set off by baby-blue eyes. A brilliant warm smile which appears often. Her body is ripe and womanly, evident even under the starched white uniform. Now she moves up on the* AIDES, *silently as though she were on wheels.*)

NURSE RATCHED. *If* you don't mind, boys? (*The* AIDES *are startled.*) I don't think it wise to group up and stand around like that. Mean ol' Monday morning, you know, *such* a lot to get done.

WARREN and WILLIAMS. Yeah, Miz Ratched.

NURSE RATCHED. That's fine, boys. Warren, you might start by getting poor Mr. Bromden shaved, and Williams, you have dormitory duty, don't you?

WILLIAMS. Yeah, Miz Ratched.

NURSE RATCHED. That's just fine. (WILLIAMS *disappears into the dormitory and* WARREN *plucks the broom from* CHIEF BROMDEN *and tows him toward the latrine.*)

NURSE FLINN. (*Enters hurriedly. She is a vapid girl with apprehensive eyes, who wears a gold cross at her throat. Breathlessly.*) Good morning, Miss Ratched. (NURSE RATCHED *looks at her watch.*) I'm sorry I'm late, but I went to Midnight Mass, and then I overslept, and—

NURSE RATCHED. (*Smilingly unlocks the Station.*) Never mind, we'd best get started, hadn't we? (NURSE FLINN *scurries into the Station and starts popping pills into paper cups.* NURSE RATCHED *throws a series of switches, then picks up the microphone. Her voice booms out over speakers in the Day Room and the dormitory.*) Medication. All patients to the Day Room. Medication. (*Clicks off the microphone. Leaves the Station, ready to greet patients as they enter. To the* FIRST PATIENT, *cheerily:*) Good morning, Mr. Harding.

HARDING. (*Pausing briefly.*) Are you sure? (*He goes to* NURSE FLINN. *He is in his late thirties, handsome, effete. Rolling his eyes aloft.*) Dear Lord, for the tranquillity we are about to receive, we thank Thee. (*Pops pills and water into his mouth. Crosses to set up a card table and get a pinochle deck from the cabinet.*)

NURSE RATCHED. (*Warmly, to the next* PATIENT.) Billy, dear. (*Linking arms with him affectionately.*) I spoke to your mother last night. (BILLY *halts apprehensively. In age, almost thirty, but appears more like a boy.*) Well, I had to tell her.

BILLY. Whu-what did you say?

NURSE RATCHED. (*Pulls back his sleeve revealing*

bandages on the wrist.) That you were very sorry and had promised not to try it again.

BILLY. Th-thank you, Miss Ratched.

NURSE RATCHED. (*Handing him his water.*) Drink it all, dear. (*Calling to another* PATIENT *who has entered.*) Good morning, Mr. Scanlon. Mr. Cheswick. (SCANLON, *a man nearly bald in his fifties, stalks across to a table without answering. He sets down a box he is carrying, pulls up a chair and starts working with tools inside the box.* CHARLES CHESWICK *is short, chubby, crew-cut; his manner alternately truculent and cringing.*)

CHESWICK. (*Examining the pills* NURSE FLINN *hands him.*) Wait a shake, honey. What're these?

NURSE FLINN. Medication.

CHESWICK. Christ, I can see *that*. What kind?

NURSE FLINN. (*Trying a flirting technique.*) Just swallow them, Mr. Cheswick—just for me?

CHESWICK. Don't gimme that crap, all I want to *know*, for the luvva God—!

NURSE RATCHED. (*Laying a hand on his arm.*) It's all right, Charles.

CHESWICK. Whattaya mean, it's all right?!

NURSE RATCHED. You don't have to take them.

CHESWICK. (*Taken aback.*) I don't? Well . . . that's okay then. (*He takes the pills and water and downs them without further fuss.* MARTINI, *a little Italian, bounds into the room, eager and bright-eyed, dashes into the latrine, immediately reappears.*)

NURSE RATCHED. Good morning, Mr. Martini.

MARTINI. (*Addressing absolutely no one.*) Mornin'! (*He goes to* NURSE FLINN *and downs his pills. Then, as* CHESWICK *has done, he joins* HARDING *and* BILLY *at the card table.* RUCKLY *enters, herded by* WILLIAMS, *shambling across stage. A once-powerful body now undirected by intelligence; blank-faced and empty-eyed, with shaven skull.*)

NURSE RATCHED. (*Greeting him.*) Mr. Ruckly.

RUCKLY. (*Pausing, his lips working in a fury of in-

articulation.) F-f-f-fuck 'em all! (*He backs into the wall as though yanked by a rubber rope, and freezes there, crucified.*)

NURSE RATCHED. (*Taking a note from her clip-board.*) Williams, we've a new admission today. I'd like you to meet him at Receiving.

WILLIAMS. (*Taking the slip of paper.*) Yeah, Miz Ratched.

NURSE RATCHED. Miss Flinn, I'll be in the Staff Room. (*To the* PATIENTS.) Behave yourself, boys! (*She exits.*)

CHESWICK. (*Mimicking.*) "Behave yourself, boys!" What choice we *got?*

(*The latrine door bursts open and* CHIEF BROMDEN *comes floundering out in flight from* WARREN *who pursues, brandishes an electric shaver with its long cord dangling.*)

WARREN. Come back here, you damn redskin! Don' like this, huh? (*He raises and brandishes it at* CHIEF BROMDEN, *making a buzzing sound, and* CHIEF BROMDEN *recoils and plops into the rocking chair, huddling in fright.*) Hmm. Can't say *I* like that look in your eye. (*Takes a restraining strap from his back pocket, skillfully whips it around* CHIEF BROMDEN'S *chest, cinching it behind the chair.*) Yeah . . . tha's some better. (NURSE FLINN *has crossed with a medical tray to* SCANLON *and now sets it down on his table.*)

SCANLON. (*Indignantly shoving the tray away from his box.*) Look out, there!

NURSE FLINN. No, no!

WARREN. (*Grinning.*) Sweet thing, you want some help?

NURSE FLINN. (*Primly.*) I don't need any, thank you. (WARREN *exits, laughing.* NURSE FLINN *retrieves her tray, and retreats to the safety of the Nurses' Station.*)

HARDING. Your deal, Martini.

MARTINI. Huh? Oh, yeah, here we go! (*Deals enthusiastically, sailing an extra set of cards off to his left to a player who isn't there.*)

CHESWICK. Hey, cut it out!

MARTINI. Whatsa matter?

CHESWICK. There's nobody there.

MARTINI. (*Looking.*) I *see* 'im.

CHESWICK. There's only *four* of us.

MARTINI. (*Doubtfully.*) Yeah? (*Picks up the cards and starts dealing again, this time sailing off an extra set to his right.*)

HARDING. Martini, will you for God's sake stop hallucinating? Oh, give me the cards! (*Snatches them and starts to deal himself.*)

CHESWICK. (*Chortling suddenly.*) Ha!

BILLY. What's f-f-funny?

CHESWICK. That mousey little nurse. Reminds me of the first time I ever saw a girl take off her clothes. I was eight, see, and I was sitting up in a tree looking through her bedroom window, and by the time she got down to her panties, I . . . I . . . (*His voice trails off as* BILLY *stands up and goes to the Log Book.*)

HARDING. (*Without turning his head.*) That's it, Billy, write it down.

BILLY. Well, we're suh-supposed to.

CHESWICK. Sure, get a gold star by your name.

BILLY. You write down everything *I* say.

CHESWICK. Yeah, and I'm going to write down some things you *did!*

HARDING. Shut up, you two.

RUCKLY. (*Roused.*) F-f-fuck 'em all!

HARDING. Oh, for heaven's sake, this place is a *madhouse!* (*Rising.*) Fellow psychopaths. As president of the Patients' Council I, Dale Harding, do hereby decree ten seconds of blessed—therapeutic—silence. (*Clasps his hands and bows his head. The silence is almost immediately shattered by a ringing, brassy voice as the ward door is opened.*)

McMURPHY. (*Off.*) Buddy, you are *so* wrong, I *don't* have to do this, and I *don't* have to do that, and *get* the hell away from me or I will take and . . . (*Has backed into view in a fighting crouch, pursued by* WILLIAMS *who looks hot and angry and frustrated. Now he becomes aware of the room and the* PATIENTS *staring at him.*) *Good* mornin', buddies! Mighty nice fall day! (*Let's have a look at* McMURPHY. *Shaggy, with long sideburns. A devilish grin and a face battered and scarred across nose and cheekbone. He wears a black motorcyclists' cap, an ancient brown leather jacket and jeans faded to almost to whiteness. On his feet lumberman's boots with a ring of steel in the heels. A wide-open, extroverted air which registers almost shockingly in this environment. Now he hooks his thumbs in his belt and starts to laugh. It rings big and free, and its vibrations jolt the* PATIENTS *open-mouthed.*) *Damn,* what a sorry-lookin' bunch!

WILLIAMS. Now, see here, mister—

McMURPHY. *Get* away from me, boy, give me a minute to look my new home over, will ya? What the hell, I never been in a Institute of Psychology before! (*As* WILLIAMS *goes into the Nurses' Station; advancing on the group.*) My name is McMurphy, buddies, R. P. McMurphy, and I am a gamblin' fool. (*Squinting at the hands.*) What's this you're playin'? Pinochle? Jesus, ain'tcha got a straight deck around here? Well, say, here we go, I brought along my own just in case. (*Distributing samples.*) Every card a picture—and check those pictures, huh? (*The* MEN *go bug-eyed at what they see on the cards.*) Fifty-two positions, boys, every one different. Easy now, *don't* smudge 'em, we got lotsa time, lotsa games. (WILLIAMS *is expostulating unheard with* NURSE FLINN *who picks up the telephone but will get no help.* McMURPHY *takes back his cards.*) Y'see, buddies, what happened was I got in a couple hassles down at the Work Farm and the Court ruled that I'm a psychopath. And do you think I'm gonna argue with the Court? (*Winks broadly.*) Shoo, you can bet your bottom dollar I don't. If it gets me outa those damn pea fields I'll be whatever their little heart desires, be it psychopath or mad dog or werewolf, because I don't care if I never see another weedin' hoe to my dyin' day— (WILLIAMS *has come up behind him to renew the assault.* MCMURPHY *seizes a chair and fends him off, lion-tamer fashion.*) —*and will you get the hell away from me?*

WILLIAMS. Mister, we got *rules.* I gotta take your temperature, and I gotta get you showered.

MCMURPHY. All you gotta do is let me get acquainted with my new buddies here, and if you do *one* thing more—!

WILLIAMS. (*Grimly.*) All right, fella, you askin' for it, you gonna get it. (*Turns and marches out of the ward.*)

MCMURPHY. (*Laughs his wall-shaking laugh.*) That's a whole deal better, now we can get somethin' settled. Okay, which of you's the bull goose loony? (*The* MEN *gape at him.*) I'm askin', who is the bull goose loony?

BILLY. Well, it's not m-me, mister. I'm not the buh-buh-bull goose loony, although you could say I'm next in luh-line for the job.

MCMURPHY. (*Sticking out his paw for* BILLY *to shake.*) Well, buddy, I'm truly glad you're next in luh-line for the job, but since I'm thinkin' a takin' over this whole shebang maybe you better take me to your leader.

BILLY. Mister Harding . . . you're President of the Pay-Pay-Patients' Council . . . .

HARDING. (*Leans back, looks at the ceiling.*) Does this . . . gentleman . . . have an appointment?

BILLY. Do you have an appointment, Mister-Mc-Muh-Murphy? Mister Harding is a busy man.

MCMURPHY. This busy man Harding, is he the bull goose loony?

BILLY. That's right.

McMURPHY. Well, you tell Bull Goose Loony Harding that R. P. McMurphy is waitin' to see him and this nut-house ain't big enough for the two of us. You tell him either he meets me man to man or he's a yaller skunk and better be outa town by sunset.

HARDING. Billy, you tell this young upstart McMurphy that I'll meet him in the main hall at high noon and we'll settle this affair once and for all, with libidos a'blazin'.

McMURPHY. Billy, you tell him that R. P. McMurphy is used to bein' top man in *every* situation, so if he's bound to be a loony he figures to be the stompdown dadgum biggest one of all! (HARDING *rises and attempts to go around* McMURPHY, *who quickly stops him by stepping in his path.* McMURPHY *holds out his hand and* HARDING, *conceding defeat, takes it.*) There, by God, and we ain't spilled a drop of blood! Now, who's the rest of these fellers?

HARDING. Well, on this side of the room we're the Acutes.

McMURPHY. What's acute about you?

HARDING. That means we are presumbly curable. Over there, the Chronics. (*Pointing out the types.*) A Walker and a Vegetable.

McMURPHY. And they ain't curable? Well, what the hell! (*Attempting to shake hands with* MARTINI.) Hiya, buddy, R. P. McMurphy, howdye do? (MARTINI *refuses to acknowledge his presence. To* CHESWICK.) Randle P. McMurphy . . .

CHESWICK. (*Ignoring his hand.*) Got any cigarettes . . . ?

McMURPHY. Nothin' butt. Get it? (*Hands him pack; shakes hands with* BILLY.) Randle Patrick McMurphy . . . (*On to* SCANLON, *a slap on the shoulder.*) Buddy, how'rya?

SCANLON. (*Slamming the lid on the box.*) Careful!

McMURPHY. What's that you're makin'?

SCANLON. (*Darkly.*) A bomb—to blow up the whole damn world.

McMURPHY. You got *competition.* (*Trots on to* RUCKLY, *pulls up short to regard him reproachfully.*) Buddy, my name is R. P. McMurphy and I don't like to see a grown man sloshin' around in his own water. Now, why'nt you go get dried up?

HARDING. Pull the nails out.

McMURPHY. The—? Oh, sure! (*Pulls the invisible "nails."*)

RUCKLY. F-f-fuck 'em all! (*He staggers off to the dorm.*)

McMURPHY. (*Stops short at* CHIEF BROMDEN *strapped in the chair.*) Hooeee! What have we got here?

CHESWICK. That's Chief Bromden.

McMURPHY. What's your story, Big Chief?

BILLY. He can't hear you. He's duh-deaf and dumb.

McMURPHY. Well, what they got him strapped down for? I don't like that, no, *sir.* (*As he unstraps the* CHIEF.) It just ain't dignified. (CHIEF BROMDEN *rises.* McMURPHY *whistles.*) Say, you get your full growth you're gonna be pretty good-sized. (*Circles* CHIEF BROMDEN *on a tour of inspection.*) What tribe is he?

BILLY. I don't know. He was here when I c-came.

HARDING. According to the doctor, he's a Columbia River Indian . . . one of those who lived up on the waterfalls? But I believe the tribe is now defunct.

McMURPHY That right, Chief? You defunct?

BILLY. He c-can't hear a word you say. (NURSE RATCHED *has entered on this, followed by* WILLIAMS. WARREN *comes out of the Station and joins them.*)

NURSE RATCHED. (*Holding out her hand.*) Mr. McMurphy.

McMURPHY. (*Shaking hands with her.*) Howdy, Ma'am!

NURSE RATCHED. I'll take that. (*She takes the strap from him, hands it to* WARREN.) Aide Williams tells me you are being difficult.

McMURPHY. (*Pained.*) Me?

NURSE RATCHED. I understand you refused to take your admission shower?

MCMURPHY. Well, as to that, ma'am, they showered me at the courthouse and last night at the jail, and I swear they'd of washed my ears for me on the way over if they coulda found the facilities. (*Explodes into laughter.*)

NURSE RATCHED. That's quite amusing, Mr. Murphy. But you must realize that our policies are engineered for *your cure*. Which means cooperation.

MCMURPHY. Ma'am, I'll cooperate from hell to Thursday, but you wouldn't want me to be unpolite? I mean, had to get acquainted with my new buddies?

NURSE RATCHED. (*Ever-smiling.*) Please understand, I *do* appreciate the way you've taken it upon yourself to . . . orient with other patients? But everything in its own time. You *must* follow the *rules*.

MCMURPHY. (*Face close to* NURSE RATCHED'S, *smiling brightly.*) Ya know, ma'am—that is the *exact* thing somebody *always* tells me about the rules—just when I'm thinkin' a breakin' every one of 'em.

(*LIGHTS DOWN FAST, but for a shaft on* CHIEF BROMDEN. *The stage does not go completely dark, but is covered by moving projections . . . bizarre, intertwining patterns through which* PEOPLE *move, slowly as in a dream, to the positions they'll occupy when the* CHIEF *has finished speaking.* NURSE RATCHED *and* WILLIAMS *go into the Station while* WARREN *exits.* SCANLON *pulls up a stool to the card table, and* MCMURPHY *sits on the back of a chair.*)

CHIEF BROMDEN. (*Voice on tape.*) New admission, Papa, now they gotta fix him with controls.

They got wires runnin' to each man and units planted in our heads.

There's magnets in the floor so we can't walk no way but what they want.

We got stone brains, cast-iron guts, and copper where they took away our nerves.

We got cog-wheels in our bellies and a welded grin,

And every time they throw a switch it turns us on or off.

They got a network clear across the land—factories, like this,

For fixin' up mistakes they made outside.

The Combine, Papa. Big, big, *big.* (*Listens a moment.*)

Oh, yes, there is *too* such a thing! They got to me way back ago. The way they got to you!

(*LIGHTS TO FULL on the Day Room. Music up simultaneously; it's miserable stuff, lawrence-welky in mode, coming from the wall speakers. In the Station* NURSE RATCHED *has replaced* NURSE FLINN *and is penciling notes in files. At the card table* MCMURPHY *is dealing Blackjack to* HARDING, CHESWICK, BILLY, SCANLON *and* MARTINI. *His cap is tilted forward until he has to lean back to see the cards. He holds a cigarette in his teeth and talks around it. His lingo sings like a pitchman's chant.*)

MCMURPHY. Heh-ya, hey-ya, come on, suckers, you hit or you sit. Hit you say? Well well well and with a king up the boy wants a hit, whaddaya know. So comin' at you, *too* bad, a little lady for the lad and he's over the wall and down the road, up the hill and dropped his load. Comin' at you, Mr. Scanlon, *and I wish some idiot in that nurses' hothouse would turn down that mother-lovin' music!* (*Rises, going toward the Station.*) Hooeee, I never heard such a drivin' racket in my life! (*Raps on the window.*)

NURSE RATCHED. (*Sliding it back.*) Yes?

MCMURPHY. Would you mind switchin' off that god-damn noise?

NURSE RATCHED. Yes, Mr. McMurphy.

McMurphy. Yes what?

Nurse Ratched. Yes, I would mind. Music is considered therapeutic.

McMurphy. What in the hell is therapeutic about Lawrence Welk?

Nurse Ratched. Please don't lean on the glass, it makes finger marks.

McMurphy. (*Turning away.*) Horse muh-noo-ur.

Nurse Ratched. Oh, Mr. Murphy, I should mention, we have a rule against gambling.

McMurphy. We're just playin' for cigarettes.

Nurse Ratched. (*Smiling.*) Are you sure those cigarettes don't represent something else?

McMurphy. Yeah, a hell of a lot of smoke. (*Laughs, then stops, noticing the* Others *are not laughing. Goes back to the table as* Nurse Ratched *closes the panel. To the* Men.) Y'know, you girls oughta laugh it up a little! (*Confidentially:*) Lissen, that was a good thing she brought up. How about we sweeten the game?

Billy. Where would we get muh-money?

McMurphy. (*Shielding the action from the Station, rubs thumb and forefinger together.*) Stop kiddin', I found out a few things about this place before I got sent over. Damn near half you boys in here pull compensation, three, four hundred a month, and it don't draw nothin' but dust. So all you gotta do is sign little IOU'S.

Harding. All right with me.

McMurphy. Let's say each cigarette's worth a dime?

Cheswick. Okay.

Scanlon. Run 'em!

McMurphy. Here we go!

Nurse Ratched. (*Over the speaker.*) Don't forget, Mr. McMurphy, no gambling for money.

McMurphy. (*Staring up at the speakers.*) Say, is that a two-way system?

Harding. No, but Miss Ratched is a human radio.

McMurphy. Is, huh? Well, I just may have to pull her plug. (*Dealing.*) All right, Professer, there you sit with a deuce showin' and here's a pack o'Marbros says you back down. (*The bell rings.*) *Now* what the hell?

Nurse Ratched. (*On Loudspeaker.*) Group Meeting. Time for Group Meeting. (*The* Men *get up quickly. The table is snatched from under* McMurphy's *elbows and chairs are arranged in a semicircle.*)

McMurphy. What's goin' *on?*

Cheswick. Group Therapy. Every day this time. (McMurphy *wanders around, puzzled. The* Acutes *take their places.* Nurse Ratched *flips a couple of switches in the Station as though setting it on automatic pilot. Picks up her wicker bag and goes to take the Log Book from its stand, then seats herself* L. *of* C., *leaving the* C. *chair vacant.*)

Nurse Ratched. Mr. Murphy, would you like to join us? (*He takes an empty chair.*) Now, then. Would anyone like to begin? (*Her eyes are on* Billy, *who at length stirs uncomfortably.*)

Billy. (*Touching the bandage on his wrist.*) I guh-guess I ought to tal' about this. (Nurse Ratched *waits.*) It was on account of my mother. Every time she comes to visit it leaves me feeling just awful.

Nurse Ratched. Your mother loves you, Billy.

Scanlon. (*Mimicking.*) Billy-darlin'. *Billy*-baby.

Billy. (*Disregarding* Scanlon.) I know. That's the trouble. I'm such a duh-disappointment to her, but she won't admit it. She won't suh-see me like I am! I say to her, "Mama, I'm nuh-not right in the head. I can't even tuh-talk straight." But she goes right on. And pretty soon I want to k-kill myself. So I try.

Nurse Ratched. Have you considered that out of your own guilt you may be trying to punish *her?*

Billy. Sure, I've considered! (*Desperately.*) Muh-Miss Ratched, couldn't we tuh-talk about somebody else today?

Nurse Ratched. You really ought to face it, Billy. (Bill *turns away, and* McMurphy *is watching in amazement. At length:*) Very well. (*She opens the Log Book.*) At the close of Friday's meeting we were discussing Mr. Harding's young wife . . . the fact that she is extremely well-endowed in the bosom. Does anyone care to touch upon this further? (*Silence, then* MCMURPHY *holds up a hand and snaps his fingers.*)

MCMURPHY. Touch upon what?

NURSE RATCHED. The subject.

MCMURPHY. Oh. I thought you meant touch upon her . . . (*Makes a mammary gesture and unleashes his laugh. But the* MEN *are gazing at him blankly and the laugh dies of malnutrition.*)

NURSE RATCHED. To continue. According to notes entered by various patients in the Log Book— (DR. SPIVEY *enters, moving fast. He is a resident psychiatrist, a pipe-smoking, glasses-fumbling, harassed fellow of no great force. He seats himself.*) —Good afternoon, Doctor.

DR. SPIVEY. Sorry. (*Makes a vague gesture, meaning "please continue," and drops his eye despondently to the floor.*)

NURSE RATCHED. Yes . . . we were talking about Mr. Harding's relations with his wife . . .

MARTINI. Whose wife? Oh. Yeah, I see her!

MCMURPHY. (*Jumping up.*) Where?

MARTINI. Mama Mia . . . !

MCMURPHY. (*Peering vainly.*) God, what I wouldn't give for that man's eyes. (DR. SPIVEY *has awakened from his stupor and is staring at* MCMURPHY. *He puts on his glasses for a better look, takes them off and turns to* NURSE RATCHED, *who calmly extracts a folder from her basket and opens it.*)

NURSE RATCHED. (*Reading.*) McMurphy, Randle Patrick. Committed by the State for diagnosis and possible treatment. Thirty-five years old. Never married. Distinguished Service Cross for leading an escape from a Communist prison camp. A dishonorable discharge afterwards for insubordination. Followed by a history of drunkenness, assault and battery, disturbing the peace, *repeated* gambling, one arrest for rape.

DR. SPIVEY. (*Perking up.*) Rape?

MCMURPHY. Statutory!

NURSE RATCHED. With a child of fifteen.

MCMURPHY. Said she was *seventeen,* and she was plenty willin'.

NURSE RATCHED. A court doctor's examination of the child—

MCMURPHY. Doc, she was *so* willin' I took to padlockin' my fly.

NURSE RATCHED. Our new admission, Doctor. (MCMURPHY *obligingly takes the folder from her and passes it to* DR. SPIVEY, *who puts on his glasses, begins reading.*)

DR. SPIVEY. Oh. Ah . . . it seems . . . you've no previous history? Any time spent in other institutions?

MCMURPHY. Well, sir, includin' state *and* county coolers—

DR. SPIVEY. *Mental* institutions.

MCMURPHY. Ah. No. This is my first trip. But I *am* crazy, Doc, I swear it. Here—lemme show you—that other doctor at the Work Farm— (*Leans over the* DOCTOR'S *shoulder, thumbing through the file.*) . . . Yeah, here it is. "*Repeated* outbreaks of passion that suggest the possible diagnosis of psychopath." He told me that psychopath means that I fight and fuck—oh, 'scuse me, how did he put it?—I'm over*zeal*ious in my sexual relations. Doc, is that real serious? I mean, you ever been troubled by it?

DR. SPIVEY. (*A little wistfully.*) No, I'll admit I haven't.

MCMURPHY. That bit about fightin' I can understand, but who ever heard of a man gettin' too much poozle?

DR. SPIVEY. (*Examining file.*) I am interested in *this* statement: "Don't overlook the possibility that this man might be feigning psychosis to escape the drudgery of the Work Farm." Well, Mr. McMurphy? What about *that?*

McMurphy. (*Turns his cap backwards; with a maniacal grin.*) Do I look like a sane man? (*Laughs with great enjoyment at this joke.*)

Nurse Ratched. Perhaps, Doctor, you should advise Mr. McMurphy on the protocol of these meetings.

Dr. Spivey. Yes. One of the first rules is that patients remain seated.

McMurphy. (*Seating himself.*) Why, sure, Doctor!

Dr. Spivey. You see, we operate on the principle of the Therapeutic Community.

McMurphy. The which?

Dr. Spivey. Ther-a-peutic Com-munity. That means that this ward is Society in miniature, and since Society decides who is sane and who isn't, you must measure up. Our goal here is a completely democratic ward, governed by the patients—working to restore you to the Outside. The important thing is to let nothing fester inside you. Talk. Discuss. Confess. If you hear another patient say something of significance, write it down in the Log Book for all to see. Do you know what this procedure is called?

McMurphy. Squealing.

Dr. Spivey. Group Therapy. Help yourself and your friends probe the secrets of the subconscious. Bring those old guilts out into the open!

McMurphy. (*Blankly.*) What guilts?

Nurse Ratched. If I may suggest, Doctor, Mr. McMurphy might learn by example? (*Re-opening the Log Book.*) According to notes entered by various patients in the Log Book, Mr. Harding has stated that he was uneasy when walking with his wife on the street because of the manner in which other men stared at her. He has further said, quote:—

Harding. (*Flat-voiced.*) She damned well gives them reason to stare, unquote.

Nurse Ratched. Yes. He has also been heard to

say that he may give *her* reason to seek sexual attention elsewhere. What reason, Dale?

HARDING. Well . . . I can't say that I have been notably ardent . . .

NURSE RATCHED. Would it be accurate to say that she finds you sexually inadequate?

CHESWICK. Maybe she's just plain too hot for him. That it, Harding?

BILLY. (*With malice out of his own hurt.*) I'll b-bet he's afraid of her.

HARDING. Not afraid!

MARTINI. Okay, scared!

HARDING. It might be fair to say . . . intimidated.

CHESWICK. Same thing.

NURSE RATCHED. I see Mr. Harding has also stated that his wife's ample bosom gives him a feeling of inferiority.

SCANLON. So why does he marry a dame with such big knockers to begin with?

CHESWICK. (*Wisely.*) I'll bet he's got a mother fixation.

SCANLON. I'll bet he was never *weaned.*

HARDING. (*Goaded . . . and* MCMURPHY *is taking it all in with growing incredulity.*) That's not so! I wanted a *womanly* woman. One who would not compete, but who might help me to . . . (*His hands wave.*)

NURSE RATCHED. To counteract certain tendencies within yourself? Would you say part of the problem is that she finds you less than masculine?

CHESWICK. Yeah, like the way you use your hands. (HARDING *captures his hands between his knees.*) How about it, Harding?

NURSE RATCHED. You chose a woman who was quite obviously your inferior. Don't you find significance in that?

HARDING. Yes, of course. But I theorized . . . it seemed to me . . . sexually, at least . . .

BILLY. Yeah. You're always saying she's such a guh-good lay.

CHESWICK. Yeah, what happens in the hay?

HARDING. Complete . . . complete psychic impotence —oh, *damn,* why do I always *cry?*

SCANLON. Say, Harding, wouldn't it be a lot easier if you was to just come out and *admit* you're a fairy?

MCMURPHY. (*Up out of his chair with a roar.*) Aw-right, knock it off!

NURSE RATCHED. Mr. Murphy!

MCMURPHY. Leave the guy alone, willya?

NURSE RATCHED. Sit *down.*

MCMURPHY. (*To* HARDING.) Lissen, buddy, you don't hafta take this shit!

NURSED RATCHED. (*Closing the Log Book with a "Splat!"*) Doctor, I suggest we close the meeting.

DR. SPIVEY. Oh?

NURSE RATCHED. Close it until *discipline* has improved. (DR. SPIVEY *obediently rises and makes his exit.* NURSE RATCHED *gathers up her paraphernalia, restores the Log Book to its podium and exits also. There is silence among the* MEN, *a subtle sense of shame at once again having betrayed one of their number.* HARDING *remains seated. His cheeks are knotted and he hums a shapeless tune.* MCMURPHY *straddles a chair facing him.*)

MCMURPHY. Say, buddy, is this the way these leetle meetings usually go? Bunch of chickens at a peckin' party?

HARDING. Pecking party? I haven't the faintest notion what you're talking about.

MCMURPHY. Why, I'll just explain it. The flock gets sight of a speck of blood on some chicken and they all go to peckin' at it, see? Till there's nothin' left but blood and bones and feathers. But usually a couple of the flock gets spotted in the fracas, then it's *their* turn.

HARDING. (*Lacing his hands together, forcing him-*

self to be casual.) A pecking party. That certainly is a pleasant analogy, my friend.

McMURPHY. That's right, my friend. And that's exactly what the meeting reminded me of.

HARDING. And that makes me the chicken with the spot of blood, eh, friend?

McMURPHY. That's right, friend. And you want to know who packs the first peck? It's that ol' nurse, that's who.

HARDING. So it's as simple as that. As stupidly simple as that. You're on our ward six hours and have already simplified the work of Freud, Jung and Maxwell Jones and summed it up in one analogy: it's a peckin' party.

McMURPHY. I'm not talkin' 'bout Fred Yoong and whosis Jones, buddy, I'm talkin' 'bout that crummy meeting and what that nurse did to you.

HARDING. Did to me?

McMURPHY. In spades.

HARDING. Why, this is incredible! You completely disregard the fact that everything she did was for my benefit.

McMURPHY. Bull-shit.

HARDING. I'm disappointed in you, my friend. I had judged you were more intelligent. But it's evident I made a mistake.

McMURPHY. The hell with you, buddy.

HARDING. Oh, yes, I also noticed your primitive brutality. Psychopath with definite sadistic tendencies, probably motivated by unreasoning egomania. And *those* talents certainly qualify you as a therapist, my friend. Oh, yes, they render you quite capable of criticizing Miss Ratched, although she's a highly regarded psychiatric nurse with twenty years' experience in the field. But you, no doubt with your talent you could work subconscious miracles, soothe the aching id and heal the wounded superego. *You* could probably cure the whole ward, Vegetables and all, in six months, ladies and gentlemen, or your money back!

McMURPHY. (*Regards him levelly.*) Are you tellin' me that this crap that went on today is doing some kinda good?

HARDING. Why else would we subject ourselves to it? Miss Ratched may be a very strict lady, but she is not some kind of monster chicken, pecking our eyes out.

McMURPHY. No, buddy. She ain't peckin' at your *eyes*. She is aimin' at a spot about three feet south—right square at the family jewels!

HARDING. Miss Ratched! Why, she's like a mother, a tender mother—

McMURPHY. Don't give me that tender-mother crap. She's sharp as a knife and twice as hard.

HARDING. (*His talk speeds up, his hands dance and flutter; a wild puppet doing a high-strung dance.*) Why, see here, my friend, my psychopathic sidekick, Miss Ratched is a veritable angel of mercy and—why, everybody knows it. She's unselfish as the wind, toiling thanklessly for the good of all, day after day, seven days a week. Why, she has no life, no husband, nothing but her work, and everybody *knows* it. Do you think she *enjoys* being stern with us, asking those questions, probing our subconscious till it hurts? Oh, no, my egomaniac buddy, she *is dedicated*, she gives every bit of herself, she desires nothing more on earth than to see us walk out of here *adjusted* and capable once more of coping with *life*. So you're wrong, I assure you. Our Miss Ratched is the kindest, sweetest, the most benevolent woman that I have . . . that I have . . . ever . . . (*Stops. Begins to laugh. And then he is crying.*) Oh, the bitch. The bitch . . . (*The* MEN *are silent.* HARDING *fumbles for a cigarette;* McMURPHY *takes it out for him and lights it.*)

BILLY. (*At length.*) You're right. About all of it.

McMURPHY. Okay, why'ntcha do something?

HARDING. Why? Because the world belongs to the strong, my friend. The rabbit recognizes the strength of the wolf, so he digs holes and hides when the wolf is about. He doesn't challenge the wolf to combat. (*Laughs.*) Mr. McMurphy . . . my friend . . . I'm not a chicken, I'm a rabbit. All of us here, rabbits, hippity-hopping through our Walt Disney world! Billy, hop around for Mr. McMurphy here. Cheswick, show him how *furry* you are. Ah, they're bashful. Isn't that *sweet?*

MCMURPHY. (*Violently.*) Shut your mouth!

HARDING. (*Quietly.*) All right, friend, what would you have us do?

MCMURPHY. Raise jack. Tell 'er to go to hell!

CHESWICK. (*Jeering.*) Try it, buddy. They'll ship you right on up to Disturbed.

SCANLON. Or down to the Shock Shop.

MCMURPHY. The which?

HARDING. Electro-Shock Therapy, my friend. A device which combines the best features of the sleeping pill, the electric chair and the torture rack.

MCMURPHY. You kiddin' me?

SCANLON. (*Touching his temples.*) Hell, no.

HARDING. (*With malicious relish.*) They strap you to a table. You are touched on each side of the head with wires. Zap! Punishment and therapy in one shocking package. Chief Broom, there. He's had two hundred treatments.

MCMURPHY. What about that little fart of a doctor?

HARDING. Oh, she requires his approval. But that's a formality. He's got two hundred patients, a bleeding ulcer and *no* desire to make waves. The *nurses* run these looney bins. (*With malice.*) What's the trouble, friend? Losing your revolutionary spirit?

MCMURPHY. What about this Democratic Ward stuff? Why'ntcha take a vote?

BILLY. What'll we v-vote?

HARDING. That the Big Nurse can't ask us any more questions?

CHESWICK. Can't look at us in a certain way?

SCANLON. Can't send us to the Shock Shop?

HARDING. (*Sweetly.*) Tell us, friend, what shall we vote?

MCMURPHY. Hell, *anything!* Don't you see you got to do something to show you still got some guts? You say the Chief is scared, but look at *you* guys. I never saw a scareder-lookin' bunch in my life!

CHESWICK. (*Standing up.*) I'm not! (MCMURPHY *turns to stare at him.* CHESWICK *sits down.*)

MCMURPHY. (*After a pause; shrugs.*) Well . . . no skin off *my* ass.

HARDING. How true.

MCMURPHY. And I sure wouldn't want some ol' fiend of a nurse after me with three thousand volts.

HARDING. Naturally.

MCMURPHY. (*On his way out.*) So what the hell.

HARDING. Oh, Mr. McMurphy. (*As* MCMURPHY *pauses; bowing.*) Welcome to the club!

MCMURPHY. (*Turning, slowly coming back.*) You say she can't do nothin' less she gets your goat?

HARDING. (*Alertly.*) That's right.

MCMURPHY. Unless she makes you crack up some way . . . like bustin' her in the nose or cussin' her out?

HARDING. You'd be safe as long as you kept your temper.

MCMURPHY. (*Walks around a little, whistling and thinking as the* MEN *watch him tensely.*) Okay. All *right.* You birds think you got the champ there. Well, how'dja like to put some *money* on it?

HARDING. On what?

MCMURPHY. That I can get the best of her.

HARDING. (*With joy.*) You propose to make a *wager* on that?

MCMURPHY. I am wagering that I can put a burr up that nurse's bloomers within a week. That I can bug her so she comes apart at them neat little seams and shows you guys she ain't unbeatable. One week, boys—and if I ain't got her where she don't know whether to shit or go blind the money is yours!

CHESWICK. (*Joyfully.*) Oh, *boy!*

MCMURPHY. Who's got five bucks they want to lose? Come on, buddies, you hit or you sit!

HARDING. Mr. McMurphy—this deserves odds. Fifteen dollars to your five that you can't do it.

MCMURPHY. (*As the* ACUTES *swarm into line, signing IOU's.*) Hey-a, hey-a, step right up, it's a spin a the wheel, a turn a the card, it's the battle a the century, one week, seven days, no holds barred, R. P. McMurphy versus the Big Nurse to a knock-out, decision or draw. Three to one is the odds, boys, getcha money down, hey-a, hey-a . . . !

MARTINI. I bet five dollars . . .

MCMURPHY. Five for the Road Runner! (NURSE RATCHED *enters.*)

NURSE RATCHED. Gentlemen, it's time for occupational therapy. (*The* ACUTES *scurry off.* WILLIAMS *takes* RUCKLY *off the wall and leads him to the dormitory.*) Mr. McMurphy? What was that activity?

MCMURPHY. (*Finishing writing down the bets.*) We're just playin' a little game.

NURSE RATCHED. You're sure it's not some form of gambling?

MCMURPHY. (*Shocked.*) Good heavens, *no,* ma'am. (NURSE RATCHED *smiles and exits.*) Gamblin', hell—this is a sure thing! (*He exits as the LIGHTS DIM DOWN FAST but for a single shaft on the* CHIEF. *Monitor lights in the Nurses' Station shift their pattern to accompaniment of electronic tonal buzzes.*)

CHIEF BROMDEN. (*Voice on tape.*) You see that, Papa? They got the place on automatic pilot for the night. It's in the night they do the things to us they want . . . things too horrible for day. And if the night ain't long enough they slow it down. Oh, yes, Papa, that's a fact. They got fake time they can speed up or slow down. I seen three months go by once in an hour. I see three days go by like this— (*A finger-snap. A cheerful whistling is heard from the dormitory. Swiftly the nightmare circuitry and sound fade out and LIGHTS bounce up to normal, night. As the* CHIEF *kneels by his rocking chair,* MCMURPHY *comes trotting in, barefoot, wearing only his denim pants and cap. He looks about, spies his pornographic deck of cards, snatches it up.*)

MCMURPHY. There y'are, babies, don't wanna lose you. (*Does a one-handed shuffle and cut, clacks the deck together and laughs in pleasure at his own dexterity. He spies* CHIEF BROMDEN.) Hey, Chief, sack time! (CHIEF BROMDEN *has upended the chair and is picking at its bottom with his fingernails.* MCMURPHY *approaches curiously.*) Whatcha doin'? (*Kneels by the* CHIEF, *whistles as he examines the lumpy bottom of the chair.*) Holy kee-rist, 'bout ten thousand pieces of gum! This where you stash it, Chief? Wait a minute, we can do better'n that. (*Digs in his pocket, triumphantly comes up with a package of gum.*) Juicy Fruit, okay? (*Unwraps the gum, sticks it in* BROMDEN'S *mouth.*) There y'are, Injun, put a nice fresh taste in your mouth. (*There is a sound of a key in the Ward door.*) Cheese it! Somebody comin'! (*Hurries to the shelter of the angle of the wall. The* CHIEF *follows. They huddle there together as* AIDE TURKLE, *the aging Negro night man, enters. Singing a little ditty,* TURKLE *puts a couple of pieces of furniture straight, checking around with his flashlight. He pulls a bottle of liquor from his back pocket and takes a couple of belts. Then he exits, singing mournfully.* MCMURPHY *and* CHIEF BROMDEN *come out of their refuge.* MCMURPHY *examines the* CHIEF *speculatively.*) Ya know, Chief . . . when I hollered, you sure did jump. I thought somebody told me you was deef? (MCMURPHY *digs a finger in the* CHIEF'S *ribs, chortles gleefully and trots into the dormitory, still laughing. The* CHIEF *follows as the LIGHTS DIM OUT.*)

(LIGHTS UP on the Day Room, empty. It is morning. AIDES WARREN *and* WILLIAMS *enter. They carry cleaning and polishing utensils and a bucket of powdered soap. They set down their materials and go to work on glass and baseboards.)*

WARREN. Finger marks an' smooches.

WILLIAMS. An' scuffs all *over* the place.

WARREN. Big Nurse see this, she raise sand fo' sure.

WILLIAMS. She beat us wi' that big brown bag.

WARREN. Haw! Why'n' we jus' beat her back?

WILLIAMS. Go, man!

WARREN. First we slug 'er with this can.

WILLIAMS. Git 'er down!

WARREN. Prize open 'er mouth!

WILLIAMS. Stuff this whole damn mess *inside*!

WARREN. Ram it to the bottom with a mop! *(They stomp the imaginary Big Nurse to death.)*

MCMURPHY. *(Off, singing.)*

"Your horses are hungry, that's what she did say,
Come sit down beside me and feed them some hay . . ."

(He comes trotting from the dormitory en route to the latrine, toothbrush in hand, wearing nothing but his cap and a towel around his hips.) Mornin', boys! *(The* AIDES *stare, less flabbergasted by his costume than by the sound of singing. Off, big and happy.)*

"My horses ain't hungry, they won't eat your ha-ay-eee,
So fare thee well, darlin', I'm gone on my way . . ."

(He comes trotting back out of the latrine and whops WARREN *on the shoulder with a big friendly hand.)* Hey, there, old buddy, what's the chance of getting some toothpaste for my grinders?

WARREN. *(Staring at the hand on his shoulder.)* We don' open the cabinet till six forty-five.

MCMURPHY. That where it is? Locked up in the cabinet?

WARREN. Tha's right.

MCMURPHY. Well well well, now why do you reckon they keep the toothpaste locked up? I mean, it ain't like it's dangerous?

WILLIAMS. (*Coming over, sniffing possible trouble.*) Ward Policy, tha's the reason.

MCMURPHY. Ward Policy? Now, why?

WILLIAMS. Well, whaddya s'pose it'd be like if everybody was to brush their teeth whenever they took the notion?

MCMURPHY. (*Reasonably.*) Uh huh, uh huh, I think I see what you're drivin' at: Ward policy is for them that can't brush after every meal.

WILLIAMS. *My gaw,* don't you *see?*

MCMURPHY. Yeah, I think I do now. You're sayin' people'd be brushin' their teeth whenever the spirit moved 'em.

WILLIAMS. Tha's right, why—

MCMURPHY. And, lordy, can you imagine? Teeth bein' brushed at six-thirty, six-twenty—maybe even six o'clock in the mornin'!

WARREN. (*Uneasily.*) C'mon, Williams. We gotta get to work . . .

MCMURPHY. Hey, wait, what do we have here?

WARREN. Where?

MCMURPHY. What's the stuff in this old can?

WARREN. Tha's soap powder.

MCMURPHY. Well, I generally use paste . . . (*Digs his toothbrush in the can, taps it on the side.*) We'll look into the Ward policy shit later. (*Goes trotting back into the latrine, singing; it becomes muffled as he brushes his teeth. The* AIDES *gape foolishly. Then* WARREN *notices* CHIEF BROMDEN, *grabs up a broom and strides over to him angrily.*)

WARREN. (*Shoving the broom in his hand.*) There, damn you, get workin', don't be gawkin' 'round like some big useless cow! Move! Move! (*The* CHIEF *is propelled into his automatic motion.* NURSE RATCHED *enters, starts to unlock the Station, freezes as she hears an alien sound.*)

McMURPHY. (*Off, singing in a lusty bellow.*)
"Oh, your parents don't like me, they say I'm too po-o-oor,
They say I'm not worthy to enter your door.
Hard livin's my pleasure, my money's my o-o-own . . .
An' them that don't like me, they can leave me alo-o-one!"
(*He has come swinging out in time to sing the last line directly to* NURSE RATCHED, *who is now staring in horror at his near-nudity.*) Good mornin', Miss Rat-shed! How's things on the outside?

NURSE RATCHED. You can't run around here . . . in a towel.

McMURPHY. Towels against Ward policy, too? Okay, I'll just . . . (*Reaches for the towel.*)

NURSE RATCHED. Stop! Don't you *dare!* (*Ominously.*) You get back in there and put your clothes on this *instant.* (*The* MEN *have entered and are watching.*)

McMURPHY. (*Hangs his head; like he's about to cry.*) I can't do that, ma'am. I'm afraid some thief in the night stole my clothes.

NURSE RATCHED. Stole . . . ? That outfit was supposed to be picked up—to be laundered. Williams?

WILLIAMS. (*Swiftly.*) Mr. Warren got laundry duty.

NURSE RATCHED. Warren. *Come here.* (WARREN *obeys fearfully.*) Couldn't you see this man had nothing on but a towel?

McMURPHY. (*Whispering.*) And my cap . . .

NURSE RATCHED. Well . . . ?

WARREN. He . . . he got up too early.

NURSE RATCHED. Got *up* too early. You'll get his clothing this instant, Mr. Warren, or spend the next two weeks on Geriatrics cleaning bedpans! (WARREN *exits, smouldering.* McMURPHY *escorts him off with a whistled few bars and a bit of soft shoe of "Sweet Georgia Brown.")* And you—get rid of that towel *at once.*

McMURPHY. Certainly! (*Whips it off. Underneath he is wearing black satin shorts with an imprint of big white whales with red eyes.* McMURPHY *grins happily.*) Ain't they some shit? (*To* EVERYONE, *displaying them.*) They was a present from a co-ed at Oregon State. She said I was some kind of symbol. (NURSE FLINN *enters and* McMURPHY *pounces on her.* NURSE FLINN *screams and runs for the Station.*)

NURSE RATCHED. Very well, Mr. McMurphy, if you've finished showing off your manly physique, I think you had better go get dressed.

McMURPHY. (*Picking up towel.*) *Dee*-lighted. (*Whacks his bare belly and sings as he goes.*)

"She took me to her parlor, and coo-ooled me with her
fan,
And whispered low in her mama's ear, I luh-uhv that
gamblin' man . . . !"

NURSE RATCHED. (*To the grinning* WILLIAMS.) Haven't you anything better to do than stand around and gape? I want this room *spotless.* (*To the* PATIENTS, *sweetly smiling.*) Gentlemen, hadn't you better get dressed? (*They scurry back into the dormitory. She goes to join* NURSE FLINN *at the Medication door.*)

NURSE FLINN. Gee, what do you think of him, Miss Ratched?

NURSE RATCHED. Mr. McMurphy?

NURSE FLINN. I mean, he's good-looking and friendly and everything, but in my opinion he just takes *over.*

NURSE RATCHED. (*Arranging a tray.*) I'm afraid that's what he's planning. And he may get away with it . . . for a while.

NURSE FLINN. Yes, but why? What would he be *after?*

NURSE RATCHED. You forget, Miss Flinn—this is an institution for the insane.

(*LIGHTS DOWN FAST but for a single shaft on the* CHIEF *as he stands holding his broom.* RATCHED *has moved into the Station, and the* PATIENTS *and* WARREN *enter, moving through the projections slow-motion. They set up chairs for Group Session, as the* CHIEF'S *thoughts are heard.*)

CHIEF BROMDEN. (*Voice on tape.*) I remember one Christmas, Papa . . . here at the hospital. It was right at midnight and there's a big wind and the door blows open whoosh! and here comes a fat man all dressed in red with a big white beard and moustache. "Ho ho ho," he says, "like to stay but I must be hurryin' along, very tight schedule, you know." Well, the Aides jumped him and pinned him down with their flashlights and gave him a tranquilizer and sent him right on up to Disturbed. They kept him six years, Papa, and when they let him go he was clean-shaved and skinny as a pole.

(*LIGHTS UP.* WARREN *enters the Station as* NURSE RATCHED *comes out. Group Meeting formation; all present except* MCMURPHY *and* DR. SPIVEY.)

NURSE RATCHED. (*Closing the Log Book.*) Now, boys, before we open the meeting I thought we might have a little discussion. Informal, you know? On the subject of Patient McMurphy.

CHESWICK. Hey, where *is* McMurphy?

NURSE RATCHED. I suggested this would be a good time for his interview with Dr. Spivey. We're not going to make any *decisions,* you understand. But I just don't think he should be allowed to go on upsetting the other patients.

SCANLON. I ain't upset.

CHESWICK. Neither am I!

NURSE RATCHED. You may not *realize* you are. However—

(*From off, a happy chortling and sounds of male good-fellowship as the Ward door opens and* DR. SPIVEY *and* MCMURPHY *enter.* MCMURPHY *has an arm about the Doctor's shoulder and they are very chummy; in fact,* MCMURPHY *takes the* DOCTOR'S *key to lock the door behind.*)

MCMURPHY. Right, Doc? Whattaya say?

DR. SPIVEY. Oh, it's a *charming* notion.

MCMURPHY. A real swingeroo! (*Digs his fingers in the* DOCTOR'S *ribs, and they laugh, poking each other.*)

NURSE RATCHED. Doctor. Doctor, we have a meeting in progress.

DR. SPIVEY. Eh? Oh sorry, go right ahead!

NURSE RATCHED. (*Smiling icily.*) Yes. We were just considering the matter of morale?

DR. SPIVEY. Why, that's exactly what *we* were talking about! And I made the suggestion . . . (*To* MCMURPHY, *puzzled.*) Or was it you?

MCMURPHY. Hell, no, it was your idea!

DR. SPIVEY. I suggested—well, what would you think if we were to have a carnival?

NURSE RATCHED. A . . . carnival?

DR. SPIVEY. (*Beaming.*) Right here on the Ward! Wouldn't it be fun? There could be games, booths, decorations . . . what do you think men?

CHESWICK. (*Galvanized by* MCMURPHY'S *big thumb.*) Oo! I think it's a *good* idea!

DR. SPIVEY. And *not* without therapeutic value.

SCANLON. Hell, yes, lots of therapeutics in a carnival!

CHESWICK. Scanlon could do his human bomb act. And I could make a ring toss in Occupational Therapy!

MCMURPHY. Myself, I'd be glad to run a Skillo

wheel. (*Chanting under the lines following.*) Heya, heya, step right up ladies and gentlemen, and try your luck, a bonanza for a dime, a prize on every spin of the wheel!

DR. SPIVEY. Oh, fine!

MARTINI. I could sell things!

HARDING. I'm rather good at palm readings.

DR. SPIVEY. Fine, fine! What do you think, Miss Ratched? (*She looks at him, frozen-smiled.*) A . . . carnival? Here on the . . . ward?

NURSE RATCHED. (*At length—letting the idea die before burying it.*) I agree it might have therapeutic possibilities. But of course it must be discussed in Staff before a decision can be reached. Wasn't that your intention, Doctor?

DR. SPIVEY. Yes, of course . . . I just thought . . . feeling out some of the patients . . but a Staff meeting . . . oh, certainly.

NURSE RATCHED. Also, Doctor, I recommend that Mr. McMurphy's request for a visitor . . . as he puts it, "A chick named Candy Starr?" . . . be denied until he becomes more familiar with the rules in this Ward.

DR. SPIVEY. I . . . well . . . Mr. McMurphy showed me his request in my office and I figured . . . I mean since he has been here a week already . . . I signed it. (MCMURPHY *and* BILLY *share* MCMURPHY'S *triumph. The* CHIEF *has put the broom back in the closet.*)

NURSE RATCHED. (*Opens the Log Book.*) I see. Very well, Billy Bibbit and his speech problem. Can you recall, Billy, when you first had speech difficulties? When did you begin to stutter?

BILLY. The v-very first word I said, I stuttered. Muh-muh-mama. And when I proposed to a guh-guh-girl, I flubbed it. I said, "Huh-huh-honey, will you muh-muh-muh . . ." (MCMURPHY *laughs companiably, and* BILLY *giggles, too.*) —till she broke out l-laughing.

NURSE RATCHED. Your mother has spoken to me about this girl, Billy. Apparently she was quite a bit beneath you. Was it that which frightened you?

BILLY. No!

NURSE RATCHED. Then what was the matter?

BILLY. I was in luh-love with her.

NURSE RATCHED. Don't you think it might have been—I'll quote from your mother, Billy— "She was a designing little slut who only wanted to marry my Billy because—"

BILLY. (*Anguished.*) No! She was a luh-lovely guh-girl that—

(*LIGHTS DOWN FAST but for a shaft on* CHIEF BROMDEN. *On sound: gunfire.*)

VOICE. Bromden!— Get that guy away from the tree before he gets shot! Bromden—Bromden—BROMDEN! Did you hear me?—Bromden, you son-of-a-bitch, did you hear me? (*Heavy artillery sounds, machine-gun fire. The* CHIEF *thrashes about in fear, then quiets as the sounds fade.*)

CHIEF BROMDEN'S VOICE. (*Over speakers.*) I can't help you, Billy. None of us can. As soon as a man goes to help somebody, he leaves himself wide open. That's what McMurphy can't understand—us wanting to be safe. That's why nobody complains about the fog. As bad as it is, you can slip back into it and feel safe.

(*LIGHTS UP FAST, FULL.*)

MCMURPHY. Say, *I* got somethin' to take up.

NURSE RATCHED. If you wish to speak you must first be recognized.

MCMURPHY. You mean you don't know me?

NURSE RATCHED. I *know* you but I don't *recognize* you.

McMURPHY. Say, you got a hell of a problem! (*Sympathetically.*) Wouldja like to discuss it?

NURSE RATCHED. Doctor, I wonder if we shouldn't discuss Mr. McMurphy?

DR. SPIVEY. In what respect?

NURSE RATCHED. I have observed a definite deterioration of discipline since he arrived. It would seem to me . . . another form of therapy . . .

McMURPHY. What you got in mind? Hookin' me up to your little battery charger?

NURSE RATCHED. (*Smiling.*) For your own good, Randle.

McMURPHY. In a pig's gizzard!

DR. SPIVEY. (*Unexpectedly.*) I must say, Nurse, I agree with Patient McMurphy. I find him quite lucid, quite in touch, and despite his past record he has exhibited no tendencies toward violence. So I must conclude that electro-shock therapy is *not* indicated.

NURSE RATCHED. Very well, if there's nothing further—

McMURPHY. Doc, I got a little matter—

MISS RATCHED. Doctor, I think you should point out that the purpose of these meetings is *therapy*, and that these petty grievances—

McMURPHY. Petty? You call the World Series petty?

DR. SPIVEY. The World Series . . . ?

McMURPHY. Sure, Doc, it starts Friday. The big games! And you got this rule about lookin' at TV only at night. Okay, let's change it to afternoon.

NURSE RATCHED. (*Sweetly.*) For therapeutic reasons?

McMURPHY. Therapeutic as all hell!

NURSE RATCHED. Or were you hoping, perhaps, to make bets on the games?

McMURPHY. How about it, guys? Don't you want to watch the Series? Cheswick?

CHESWICK. Why not?

McMURPHY. Scanlon?

SCANLON. (*Uneasily.*) I don't know, Mac . . .

NURSE RATCHED. Mr. Scanlon, as I recall, you refused to eat for three days until we allowed you to turn the set on at six instead of six-thirty.

SCANLON. A man needs to see the news, don't he? God, they coulda bombed us clear to hell and it'd be a week before we knew. (*To* NURSE RATCHED.) Can't have both, huh?

NURSE RATCHED. No, you definitely cannot.

SCANLON. Well . . . I guess maybe they won't bomb us this week.

MCMURPHY. Attaboy! Let's take a vote. All those in favor raise your hands! (CHESWICK'S *hand comes up. And* SCANLON'S. *The* OTHER MEN *look at the floor.*) Hey, what is this crap? I thought you guys could vote on stuff like this. Ain't that right, Doc? (*The* DOCTOR *nods.*) Okay, then, who wants to watch those games? (CHESWICK'S *hand goes higher but there is no other response.*) What's the *matter* with you guys?

NURSE RATCHED. Three, Mr. McMurphy. Just three. Not sufficient to change Ward Policy. Now, if that's settled may we terminate the meeting?

MCMURPHY. Yeah . . . let's terminate the lousy meeting.

(DR. SPIVEY *rises and exits.* NURSE RATCHED *replaces the Log Book and exits. The* PATIENTS *put the chairs back, then scatter about the room.* WARREN *helps, then returns to the Station.*)

BILLY. (*Finally.*) Listen, Randle. Some of us have b-been here a long time. And some of us will b-be here a long time after you're gone. A l-long time after the World Series is over. And don't you see . . . d-don't you realize . . .

MCMURPHY. (*Shaking his head.*) I don't understand it. I—don't—understand—it. (BILLY *turns away in despair.*) Harding, what's the matter with you?

(HARDING *shrugs, turns away.*) What are you guys afraid of? Why, you bunch of gutless wonders. I oughta just leave you to her. Yeah, that's what I oughta do—bust on outa here and nail the door shut behind.

BILLY. Yeah? All right, you're talking so big, just how would you break out?

MCMURPHY. Forty ways!

HARDING. Name *one.*

MCMURPHY. You think I'm kidding, huh? (*Looks about, and his eyes light on the chest-like panel at the foot of the Station.*) There. That thing Billy's sittin' on. I could throw it through that mesh window.

HARDING. I don't recall anything about psychopaths being able to move mountains.

MCMURPHY. Hell, are you tellin' me I can't *lift* that dinky thing?

HARDING. That dinky thing weighs half a ton. *And* it contains all the electrical equipment for the Station.

SCANLON. Hell, yes, try it, Mac. You'll short-circuit the controls and blow this whole damn hospital into orbit! (*Makes a gesture of giving "The Finger" to* HARDING.)

MCMURPHY. Who's willin' to lay five bucks?

HARDING. This is more foolhardy than your bet against Big Nurse.

MCMURPHY. Five bucks, you peckerheads! 'Cause nobody's gonna convince me I can't do anything till I try. Here—all your IOU'S from Blackjack. (*Slamming them on the table.*) I'll put up the whole shebang, double or nothin'!

HARDING. You're on!

OTHER MEN. Covered! I'll take it! Etc.

MCMURPHY. Stand back, boys. Scanlon, get the women and children someplace safe! (MCMURPHY *tries, but the box doesn't budge.*)

SCANLON. Ah, Mac, you giving up . . . ?

MCMURPHY. Hell, no. Just *warmin'* up. Here goes the real effort! (*This time he throws all his strength into it. He closes his eyes and his lips strain away from his teeth. His head is thrown back, his whole body shaking with the strain.* CHIEF BROMDEN *finds himself moving toward* McMURPHY *in a sort of muscular empathy. The air explodes out of* McMURPHY'S *lungs. He collapses over the panel and sags to the floor. For a few moments there is no sound but his scraping breath. Then he pulls himself to his feet, crosses and picks up the IOU's with clawed and shaking hands. Proffers them but no one makes a move, so he strews them on the floor. Turns and makes his way unsteadily toward the dormitory.*)

HARDING. Mac. (McMURPHY *pauses.*) *No* man could lift that thing.

McMURPHY. (*Turning; there are tears of rage and frustration in his eyes.*) But I tried. Goddamnit, I *tried.* (*Exits into the dormitory.* CHIEF BROMDEN *follows a step or two, his arms reaching out. LIGHTS DOWN FAST except for a shaft on* CHIEF BROMDEN *as the* MEN *exit.*)

CHIEF BROMDEN. (*Voice on tape.*) I want to touch him. I want to touch him so I can help him. That's a lie. I want to touch him because I'm one a them queers. No, that's a lie too . . . if I was a queer I'd wanta do other things with him. I just want to touch him . . . (*LIGHTS TO FULL.* AIDE WILLIAMS *is crossing to hand* CHIEF BROMDEN *his broom.*)

WILLIAMS. Awright, work time, *get* goin'. (*The* PATIENTS *engage in jobs of floor polishing, dusting, etc.*)

(WILLIAMS *closes the* CHIEF'S *hands around the broom handle, starts him moving like an automaton.* NURSE RATCHED *enters the Station. We hear a snatch of singing—*McMURPHY'S *voice—from within the latrine.* WILLIAMS *goes to peer through the latrine's window in suspicion. Suspicion verified; he marches across to the Station and taps on the glass.* NURSE RATCHED *slides back the panel, frowns at what* WILLIAMS *mumbles in* *her ear. She comes out of the Station and crosses to the latrine.)*

NURSE RATCHED. (*Rapping on the door.*) Mr. McMurphy, *Mr. McMurphy.*

MCMURPHY. (*Sticking his head out.*) Ma'am?

NURSE RATCHED. Would you step out here, please?

MCMURPHY. (*Emerges, a toilet mop in hand.* NURSE RATCHED *brushes by him and enters the latrine.*) Boy, she musta had to go in a hurry!

NURSE RATCHED. (*Emerging, very angry.*) Mr. McMurphy, that is an outrage.

MCMURPHY. (*Firmly.*) No ma'am, that is a latrine.

NURSE RATCHED. You are supposed to get those fixtures *clean.*

MCMURPHY. Well, ma'am, they might not be clean enough for some people, but me, I'm plannin' to piss in 'em, not eat lunch out of 'em.

NURSE RATCHED. I think we'd better give you another job. (*Enters Station.*)

MCMURPHY. (*Slapping the wet brush onto* WILLIAMS' *chest.*) Take over, buddy! (WILLIAMS, *in fury, takes mop to the broom closet, then enters Station. To the* MEN.) You guys ready to pay off them IOU's?

HARDING. You haven't won yet, friend! (MCMURPHY *goes to* CHIEF BROMDEN, *takes a stick of gum from his pocket.*)

MCMURPHY. (*Singing.*)

"Oh, does the Spearmint lose its flavor on the bedpost overnight,
When you chew it in the mornin' will it be too hard to bite?"

(*Laughs happily and sneaks the piece of gum into the* CHIEF'S *hand.*)

WARREN (*Entering.*) Visitor, Mr. McMurphy. (CANDY STARR *enters.*)

CANDY. McMurphy.

MCMURPHY. *Candy baby!*

CANDY. Oh, you damned McMurphy! (*Runs to*

him, leaps into his arms. They kiss—sensationally—and heads swivel toward them. NURSE RATCHED *clicks on the microphone.*)

NURSE RATCHED. Please identify your visitor.

MCMURPHY. (*Bellowing.*) She's my goddam mother! (*To the* MEN.) Buddies, this is Candy Starr.

CANDY. (*Turns to them, smiling.*) Hiya, boys, how's every little thing? (*To* SCANLON.) Hey, Pop, what they got you in for?

SCANLON. Rape.

MCMURPHY. (*Laughs.*) Honey, this is Billy Bibbit. Wouldja believe it? He's a virgin.

CANDY. (*With instant sympathy, taking* BILLY'S *hand.*) Aw, they lock you up for *that?*

MCMURPHY. Come on over here and talk to me. (*Sits with her on a couch, and* BILLY, *fascinated, draws close.*) How's Sandra?

CANDY. Tied up, man, I mean like *really*. She got married.

MCMURPHY. Got which?

CANDY. (*Giggling.*) Can you feature that? Ol' Sandy married.

MCMURPHY. Wow! Who to?

CANDY. You remember Artie, from Beaverton? Always used to show up at the parties with some gassy thing, a gopher snake or a white rat or some gassy thing like that? Jesus, a real maniac! (*She claps a hand over her mouth and looks at the* MEN, *roundeyed.*)

MCMURPHY. That's okay, honey, they're a lot crazier outside.

CANDY. You damned McMurphy . . . (*Throws her arms about his neck. The LOUDSPEAKER clacks on.*)

NURSE RATCHED. (*On microphone.*) Mr. McMurphy—

MCMURPHY. (*Raising both hands.*) Okay!

CANDY. Are you all right, baby? I mean, they treating you all right?

MCMURPHY. Oh, hell, yes. The grub—sensational.

And the bed they give a man . . . hey, why'n't I show you the dormitory?

CANDY. (*Hopping to her feet.*) Why not? (MCMURPHY *takes her by the hand and is leading her toward the dormitory when the LOUDSPEAKER clacks on again.*)

NURSE RATCHED. Mr. McMurphy—

MCMURPHY. (*Reversing course.*) Okay, *okay.* (*Comes back into dayroom, makes* X *to indicate exact spot, yells to* RATCHED.) Here . . . ? Here . . . ? (*To* CANDY.) I think she wants to watch. (*Grabs* CANDY *in an embrace. Then, low:*) Listen, honey, I got an idea. You talking about the old parties and all . . . I bet I could fix it so we could throw one right here.

CANDY. (*And some of the* MEN *inch closer, listening.*) You kiddin'?

MCMURPHY. And maybe you could bring Sandra.

CANDY. I told you, ol' Sandy got married.

MCMURPHY. Well, she still digs parties?

CANDY. Oh, sure! But . . . how'd we get in? (MCMURPHY *looks about, beckons her closer, whispers rapidly in her ear as the* MEN *draw toward them.* CANDY *giggles delightedly.*) What an absolute gas! (*She jumps into his arms.*)

NURSE RATCHED. (*On microphone.*) Mr. McMurphy—I'm afraid you'll have to ask your visitor to leave.

CANDY. (*In protest.*) Hey, I just got here!

MCMURPHY. (*With a big wink.*) Later, baby. Say so long to the fellows.

CANDY. (*Clinching with him.*) You damned McMurphy! (*To the* MEN.) Later, boys.

MCMURPHY. Nice kid. Comes from a good family.

BILLY. (*Bursting out.*) You're not really guh-going to do it?

MCMURPHY. Why not?

SCANLON. A party *here?*

MCMURPHY. That's the caper.

BILLY. With C-Candy?

MCMURPHY. Cute trick, huh? How'd you like to bump bellies with *that?*

BILLY. (*Overcome.*) Oh, b-b-boy!

HARDING. My friend, for pure audacity that proposition wins the analysts' Oscar.

MCMURPHY. I plan to fling the greatest brawl that ever got flung in a loony-bin.

MARTINI. (*Clapping his hands joyfully.*) Oh, man, we're gonna have a party!

MCMURPHY. (*Springing the trap.*) We? Who the hell said we?

HARDING. We're not invited?

MCMURPHY. Nope.

BILLY. (*Dismayed.*) But why?

MCMURPHY. 'Cause I'm fed up with you jerks, that's why! Runnin' scared from a female woman! Know what's goin' on this very minute? The World Series! And *you* gutless wonders kept me from seein' it!

CHESWICK. But, Mac, we tried.

MCMURPHY. Sure, you and Scanlon. All the rest too damn scared to raise their hands!

HARDING. I'm sorry, Mac. If the matter weren't already closed . . .

MCMURPHY. Anything in the rules say you can't vote again?

HARDING. N-no, I don't recall that there is.

MCMURPHY. Well, then?

NURSE RATCHED. (*Has come out of the Station and approached the* GROUP. WILLIAMS *follows.*) Haven't you gentlemen work to do?

MCMURPHY. (*Boldly.*) Sure, but right now we got a special meeting of the Patients' Council.

NURSE RATCHED. Called by whom?

MCMURPHY. Mister Dale Harding, President!

HARDING. (*A pause, then unsteadily, as* NURSE RATCHED *turns her eyes on him.*) That's right, Miss Ratched.

NURSE RATCHED. For what purpose?

HARDING. For . . . for . . .

MCMURPHY. For the purpose a takin' a re-vote on changing TV time to afternoon!

NURSE RATCHED. I see.

MCMURPHY. Okay, boys—!

NURSE RATCHED. One moment! Do any of you feel, perhaps, that Mr. McMurphy is imposing his personal desires on you? I've been thinking you might be happier if he were moved to another ward.

SCANLON. You can't send him to Disturbed just for bringin' up a vote!

CHESWICK. (*Defiantly.*) That's right.

NURSE RATCHED. (*To* MCMURPHY.) You're certain one more vote will satisfy you?

MCMURPHY. I just wanta see once and for all which of these birds has any guts and which hasn't.

NURSE RATCHED. Very well. Everyone in favor of changing television time to afternoon, raise your hands. (*The hands come up . . .* BILLY'S *a little slower than the others. Finally all are raised but the* CHIEF'S.)

MCMURPHY. (*Racing toward the TV set.*) Batter up!

NURSE RATCHED. One moment, please! The rules call for a unanimous vote.

MCMURPHY. Unanimous . . . ? (*Catches on, points to* BROMDEN *in disbelief.*) You mean you want the Chief to vote? (BROMDEN *moves to the closet to deposit his broom; enters the closet, pulling the door shut behind him.*)

HARDING. (*Nods his head miserably.*) All the patients present on the ward.

MCMURPHY. So *that's* how you work this democratic bull. Of all the crummy things I ever heard—!

NURSE RATCHED. (*Calmly.*) You seem upset, Mr. McMurphy. I'll have to make a note of that.

MCMURPHY. Hold on—!

NURSE RATCHED. The meeting is closed.

McMURPHY. (*Frantically.*) Hold on one lousy *minute.* (*Looks for the* CHIEF, *goes to the closet, opens door.*) Chief, Chief . . . (*Pulls* CHIEF *out by the back of his shirt.*) Chief, come on out here. Chief, it's now or never. We're men or we're monkeys, we make or we break. Get your hand up right *now.*

NURSE RATCHED. Don't be ridiculous, the poor man can't even hear you.

McMURPHY. Come on, Chief, get that hand up and *vote.* (*All eyes on the* CHIEF. *After a moment* McMURPHY *gives up. In frustration, he slams his cap to the floor, sits in the rocking chair as the* OTHERS *return to their work.* RATCHED *goes back to the Station. The* CHIEF *begins to raise his hand.*)

CHESWICK. (*Noticing.*) Mac . . . !

WILLIAMS. (*Also noticing.*) Miss Ratched . . .

McMURPHY. (*Jumping up, pointing to the* CHIEF *exuberantly.*) Unanimous! (*The* MEN *explode into action, setting chairs and wheeling the TV set into position, etc.* NURSE RATCHED *is staring at* CHIEF BROMDEN. *Taking the* CHIEF *by the hand.*) Sid-down, you gorgeous monster, best damn seat in the house!

SCANLON. Okay, let 'er rip! (NURSE RATCHED *turns abruptly and goes into the Nurses' Station.*)

ANNOUNCER'S VOICE. (*As* CHESWICK *adjusts the TV.*) . . . and he swings! At a bad pitch, oh my, and the count is three and two with the tying run on second base. It's the bottom of the sixth . . . a hit and run situation . . . here comes the windup. It's a— (*In the Station* NURSE RATCHED *has opened a panel on the wall behind the desk, and thrown a switch. The TV cuts off abruptly.* McMURPHY *comes to his feet.*)

NURSE RATCHED. (*On microphone.*) The meeting was *closed.* (McMURPHY *starts toward her.*)

HARDING. (*A warning.*) Mac.

NURSE RATCHED. You men will now go back to your duties. (*No one moves.*) Did you hear me? (*The* MEN *start to move.*)

MCMURPHY. Don't move. Billy—sit down. (*They go back to their chairs.*)

NURSE RATCHED. *Did you hear me?* (*The* MEN *break and go back to their duties.* MCMURPHY *holds his position.*)

MCMURPHY. (*Finally, turning to TV set.*) Hoo, boy, lookit that. It's a hit. Right down the middle!

HARDING. (*Catching on, looks at* NURSE RATCHED, *wavers. Finally sits back down.*) Run, you mother-loving turkey, *run!*

MARTINI. (*Resumes his place.*) Two bases, *two.* Look out, there comes the throw!

SCANLON. He missed it! Overthrew second!

MCMURPHY. Keep goin', for the luvva God, keep goin'!

NURSE RATCHED. (*Coming out of the Station.*) Stop it. *Stop* it.

CHESWICK. Take another! Take another base!

NURSE RATCHED. (*Standing between them and TV.*) Stop it, I tell you! You men are under my jurisdiction . . . my jurisdiction and *control—*

HARDING. He dropped the ball!

BILLY. There it g-g-goes—!

HARDING. Into the outfield!

MCMURPHY. All the way home, you jerk! Run, run, run!

NURSE RATCHED. You men stop it! Mr. Harding! Mr. Cheswick! (*Her voice is drowned out in the shouting.*)

MCMURPHY. (*Quelling the noise.*) Oh, Nursie—wouldja mind bringin' me a red-hot and a can a beer?

CHESWICK. HOME RUN!!! (*The* MEN *burst into cheers of triumph.* NURSE RATCHED *is shouting at them, unheard, out of control.*)

CURTAIN

END OF ACT ONE

ACT TWO

The Dayroom is empty but for RUCKLY, *who stands atop the panel, arms extended with fingers touching, hoop fashion. The shrilling of a referee's whistle, and* MCMURPHY *comes charging out, followed by* HARDING, CHESWICK, SCANLON *and* MARTINI. *They wear underwear in simulation of gym shorts, and are dribbling and passing a basketball.* CHIEF BROMDEN *follows, hovering on the outskirts of the action as though he would like to join in. Two or three baskets are shot through* RUCKLY'S *"hoop" to the accompaniment of joyful yapping.*

MCMURPHY. *Snap* the ball. Use your elbows, willya? Drive, you puny mothers, *drive.* (*Blows the whistle, stopping action.*) Ruckly, how many times have I got to tell you, stand *still.* It ain't right for the basket to be chasin' the ball. (*He blows his whistle and they resume play.* MARTINI *tosses the ball to an imaginary teammate.*)

MARTINI. Hey, George! (MCMURPHY *blows the whistle, retrieves the ball.*)

MCMURPHY. Martini. There's only five men on a team. One . . . two . . . three . . . four . . . five. So don't go hallucinatin' any more!

(*Suddenly—LIGHTS DOWN FAST but for a shaft on* CHIEF BROMDEN, *and all others FREEZE. There is a flowing PROJECTION and the sound of rushing water.*)

CHIEF BROMDEN. (*Voice on tape.*) There! The waterfall! How come I hear it, Papa, when it's miles and years away? I hear it and it sounds like in the

Spring. I see a salmon jump! I smell the snow where the wind is blowin' off the peaks! And there's the Tribe out there above the falls. Listen the way they yell each time they spear a fish! How come, Papa? It all got lost when I was still a kid . . . what's makin' it come back?

(*LIGHTS UP FAST. Action as before; the ball being passed to much yipping and yapping, as though there had been no pause.* AIDE WILLIAMS *enters, stops short in consternation.*)

WILLIAMS. Hey! You can't play basketball in here.

MCMURPHY. Why not? Ah-ha, don't tell me . . . against ward policy?

WILLIAMS. (*Grabbing the ball.*) You got it, buddy.

MCMURPHY. Aw, shucks, just when we got an alumni game comin' up. (NURSE FLINN *has entered and is observing, in shock.* MCMURPHY *goes toward her.*) Hiya, honey! (*Reaching for the crucifix she wears about her throat.*) Mind if I take a look at that thing?

NURSE FLINN. (*Backing away.*) Oh, stay back!

MCMURPHY. Honey, I just wanta *look* at it.

NURSE FLINN. (*Pleadingly.*) Please . . .

MCMURPHY. I swear I ain't gonna hurt you, I just wanta—

RUCKLY. F-f-fuck 'em all!

NURSE FLINN. (*Shrieking.*) Don't touch me, I'm a *Catholic!* (*The Ward door opens.* WARREN *enters, followed closely by* NURSE RATCHED. ALL *are frozen by her presence as she takes in the scene.* WILLIAMS *looks, foolishly, from her to the basketball in his hands.*)

NURSE RATCHED. (*To* WILLIAMS.) Good game? (*To* WARREN.) Please take Mr. Ruckly down. (WARREN *lifts* RUCKLY *down and stands him in his accustomed place against the wall.* NURSE RATCHED *takes the basketball from* WILLIAMS. *Moving on to* MCMUR-

PHY; *goodnaturedly.*) We do have our little difficulties, don't we? But they'll be worked out. After all, we have weeks. Months. If necessary, years. (*She exits, followed by* WARREN *and* WILLIAMS, *as* FLINN *hurries into the Station. The* MEN *break into a hubbub, crowding around* McMURPHY.)

CHESWICK. You've got her on the ropes!

SCANLON. She's groggy, Mac!

McMURPHY. Yeah . . .

HARDING. All you need is the knockout punch!

BILLY. I wouldn't have believed it—!

McMURPHY. Shut up, will ya? Wha'd she mean by that?

CHESWICK. What, Mac?

McMURPHY. That "years" bit. (*Silence.*) Come on, why does she act like she's still holdin' the aces?

HARDING. Well . . . I guess maybe it's because you're committed.

McMURPHY. Sure I'm committed, but my sentence only got five months to run, so . . . (*Looks at the faces. They are uneasy, some showing a kind of guilt.*) Come on, gimme the bit.

HARDING. Mac, it's not like a jail sentence. In jail you've got a date ahead when you know you'll be set free. But here . . . if you're committed . . .

McMURPHY. You mean I'm stuck here till she wants to turn me loose? (HARDING *is silent.* McMURPHY *is badly jolted.*) Hey . . . then I got as much to lose hasslin' that ol' buzzard as *you* do.

HARDING. More. I'm voluntary.

McMURPHY. You're which?

HARDING. I'm not committed. As a matter of fact, there aren't many on the ward who are.

McMURPHY. Are you bulling me? (HARDING *shakes his head.*) Are you guys bulling me? (*No answer, but the* MEN *shift around uneasily.*) Billy—*you* must be committed? (BILLY *shakes his head.*) Then why? Why? You're just a young kid. Why ain't you out runnin' around in a convertible, bird-doggin' girls?

(BILLY *looks down at the floor.*) All you guys, why the hell do you *stay?* You gripe, you bitch how you can't stand this place, can't stand the Big Nurse, and here all the time you ain't *committed!* What's the *matter* with you? Ain't you got any guts?

BILLY. Sure! Sure, that's it, we haven't got the guts! I could g-g-get out this afternoon if . . . (*Wildly.*) You think I wuh-want to stay in here? Sure, I'd like a convertible and a guh-girl friend. But did you ever have people l-l-laughing at you? No, because you're so big and tough. Well, I'm not big and tough. Neither is Harding. Neither is Cheswick. Oh—oh, you—you t-talk like we stayed in here because . . . oh . . . what's the use . . .

MCMURPHY. (*Hard.*) Okay, why didn't you tell me?

HARDING. What?

MCMURPHY. That she could keep me here till my dyin' day.

HARDING. I guess . . . it didn't occur to us.

MCMURPHY. That's a lotta crap! Oh, now I get it. Now I see why you guys keep comin' at me like I'm Jesus Q. Christ. It's 'cause I got everything to lose, and you . . . hooee, how d'you like that? You bastards conned me. Conned by a bunch of wackos!

HARDING. Mac, believe me—

MCMURPHY. To hell with that. To hell with *you.* I got plenty of worries of my own without gettin hooked on yours. So quit buggin' me. (*A yell.*) Alla you! Quit *buggin' me!* (*A stunned silence. He makes a decision, goes to the broom closet, opens it and takes out the toilet brush.* NURSE RATCHED *enters with the* AIDES, *pauses as she sees* MCMURPHY *emerge from the closet and start toward the latrine.*)

NURSE RATCHED. Mr. McMurphy. (*He stops as she comes to him.*) What are you planning to do with that?

MCMURPHY. Plannin' to use it, ma'am. Plannin' to scrub them urinals so clean we're gonna have to wear dark glasses every time we take a pee. (*Goes into the latrine.*)

NURSE RATCHED. (*Examining the* MEN *thoughtfully.*) Mr. Harding.

HARDING. (*Low.*) Yes, Miss Ratched?

NURSE RATCHED. Have you gentlemen been reasoning with Mr. McMurphy?

HARDING. Yes, Miss Ratched.

NURSE RATCHED. Just what did you say?

HARDING. We . . . explained the Therapeutic Community.

NURSE RATCHED. I see. (*She smiles.*) That's fine, boys. That's just fine.

(*GENERAL DIMOUT. MUSIC BRIDGES. Then LIGHTS UP to night lighting on the empty Day Room. The Nurses' Station is faintly illuminated from within. Elsewhere there are only the blue nightlights; and moonlight pours through the windows. For a few moments the stage is deserted. Then* CHIEF BROMDEN *enters from the dormitory. He looks about in a puzzled way as though someone had called to him. He is drawn to the windows, magnetized by moonlight. Raises his head looking up at the sky . . . and in the hush is heard the high laughing gabble of wild geese passing overhead. He raises his arms wide, as though to embrace the whole lost world beyond the windows, then folds them about his body. He is standing like that, head thrown back, eyes closed, when* MCMURPHY *enters.*)

MCMURPHY. (*Whispering.*) Chief, you all right? (*No acknowledgment.*) Saw you get up and figgered maybe you come out here to scrape off some a that thousand-year gum. (*Offering a stick of gum; apologetically.*) They took away my canteen privileges so this is all I got.

CHIEF BROMDEN. (*Taking it—then he speaks in a hoarse voice.*) Thank you.

MCMURPHY. That's okay. (*Starts off, comes to a startled halt.*) Hey—! (*Coming back.*) Try it again—you're a little rusty.

CHIEF BROMDEN. (*Clears his throat; more clearly.*) Thank you. (MCMURPHY *starts to laugh, trying to keep the sound down.* CHIEF BROMDEN *goes toward the dormitory, his feelings hurt.*)

MCMURPHY. (*Stopping him.*) 'Scuse me, Chief. What I was laughin' at, I just caught wise to what you been doin' all these years—bidin' your time till you could tell 'em off!

CHIEF BROMDEN. No . . . no, I'd be afraid.

MCMURPHY. How's that?

CHIEF BROMDEN. I'm not big enough.

MCMURPHY. Hoo boy, you *are* crazy, aren't you. I been on a few reservations in my life, but you are the *biggest* damn Injun I have ever seen!

CHIEF BROMDEN. My papa was bigger.

MCMURPHY. Yeah?

CHIEF BROMDEN. He was a full chief and his name was Tee Ah Millatoona. That means The Pine That Stands Tallest on the Mountain. But my mother got twice his size.

MCMURPHY. You must of had a real moose of an old lady!

CHIEF BROMDEN. Oh, she wasn't big *that* way. She wasn't Indian, neither. She was a town woman. Her name was Bromden.

MCMURPHY. Yeah, I think I see what you're gettin' at . . . when a town woman marries an Indian that's marryin' beneath her, ain't it? And your papa had to take her name?

CHIEF BROMDEN. She said she wouldn't be married to no man with a name like Tee Ah Millatoona. But it wasn't only her that made him little. Everybody worked on him. The way they're workin' on you.

McMurphy. They who?

Chief Bromden. The Combine. It wanted us to go live some place else. It wanted to take away our waterfall. In town they beat up Papa in the alleys and cut off his hair. Oh, the Combine's big . . . big. He fought it a long time till my mother made him too little to fight any more. Then he signed the papers.

McMurphy. What papers, Chief?

Chief Bromden. The ones that gave everything to the government. The village. The falls . . .

McMurphy. I remember . . . but I heard the tribe got paid some huge amount.

Chief Bromden. That's what the government guys said, here's a whole big pot of money. And Papa said, what can you pay for the way a man lives? What can you pay for his right to be an Indian? They didn't understand. Neither did the tribe. They stood in front of our door, holdin' those checks, askin' what should we do now? And Papa couldn't tell them 'cause he was too little . . . and too drunk.

McMurphy. What happened to him?

Chief Bromden. He kept drinkin' till he died. They found him in a alley and threw dirt in his eyes. (*Fiercely.*) The Combine whipped him. It beats *everybody.*

McMurphy. Now, wait a minute—

Chief Bromden. Yes, yes, it does! Oh, they don't bust you outright. They work on you, ways you can't even see. They get hold of you and they *install* things!

McMurphy. Take 'er easy, buddy.

Chief Bromden. And if you *fight* they lock you up some place and make you stop and—!

McMurphy. (*Closing the* Chief's *mouth with his hand.*) Woops, cool it. (*Takes him in his arms, gently, soothingly.*)

Chief Bromden. (*In a moment, ashamed.*) I been talkin' crazy.

McMurphy. Well . . . yeah.

Chief Bromden. It don't make sense.

McMurphy. I didn't say it didn't make sense.

Chief Bromden. Sh-h! (*Raises his head, moves toward the windows, listening.*) Hear 'em? (McMurphy *comes to him, listens. From the sky the wild, gabbling cry again.*)

McMurphy. Canada honkers flyin' south. Gonna be an early winter, Chief. Look, there they go. Right across the moon!

Chief Bromden. (*Gazing skywards, chanting softly.*) Wire, brier, limber lock . . .

McMurphy. Huh?

Chief Bromden. It's a old children's rhyme. My grandmomma taught it to me . . .

McMurphy. Oh, lord, yes, I remember! You play it with your fingers. Hold out your hand, Chief. (*Ticking off fingers, chanting.*) Wire, brier, limber lock—

Chief Bromden. Three geese in a flock.

McMurphy. One flew east—

Chief Bromden. One flew west—

McMurphy. An' one flew over the cuckoo's nest!

Chief Bromden. O-U-T spells out—

McMurphy. Goose swoops down and plucks *you* out! (*They embrace, laugh happily; then the* Chief *sobers.*)

Chief Bromden. McMurphy?

McMurphy. Yeah?

Chief Bromden. You gonna crawfish? (McMurphy *doesn't answer.*) I mean, you gonna back down?

McMurphy. (*Turning away.*) Aw . . . what's the difference?

Chief Bromden. Are you?

McMurphy. (*His eyes light on the panel. Brightly:*) Hey, remember when I tried to lift that thing? I bet *you* could do it.

Chief Bromden. (*Shrinking back.*) I'm too little.

McMurphy. Whyn't you give it a try?

Chief Bromden. I'm not *big* enough!

McMurphy. How do ya know? That'd be one sure way to find out. (*Giving up, cheerfully.*) Well, when you're ready, lemme make book on it. Hoo boy, would *that* be a killin'!

CHIEF BROMDEN. McMurphy. (MCMURPHY *pauses.*) Make me big again.

MCMURPHY. Why, hell, Chief . . . looks to me like you growed half a foot already!

CHIEF BROMDEN. (*Shaking his head.*) How can I be big if you ain't? How can anybody? (*He exits into the dorm.* MCMURPHY *is motionless a moment, then follows.*)

(*The LIGHTS DIM OUT. LIGHTS UP, daylight.* NURSE FLINN *is in the Station.*)

NURSE FLINN. (*Picking up microphone.*) Council meeting. Patients' Council meeting. (MARTINI *rushes from the dormitory in the midst of a frantic hallucination.*)

MARTINI. Air to ground . . . air to ground! . . . Enemy sighted at three o'clock! Enemy planes at three o'clock. (*He wildly fires his imaginary machine gun into the sky.*)

CHESWICK. (*Coming out of latrine.*) Knock it off, Martini. There's no one there.

MARTINI. (*Excitedly.*) Don't you see them? Don't you see them?

CHESWICK. There's no one there, I tell you. Now stop it. There's no one there . . . (*He takes* MARTINI *in his arms and quiets him.*)

MARTINI. (*Sadly.*) I thought I seen them. (*The others enter. Their attitude is subdued, brooding. The* CHIEF *sits in the rocking chair.* MCMURPHY *enters, head down, and seats himself, too.* WARREN *and* WILLIAMS *enter with almost military precision, preceding* NURSE RATCHED.)

NURSE RATCHED. Boys, I've given a great deal of thought to what I am about to say. I've talked it over with the Staff and we all came to the same conclusion—that there should be some form of punishment for the unspeakable behavior of yesterday. (*A pause. No comment.*) Most of you are here because you could not adjust to the outside world. You broke the rules of society. At some time . . . in your childhood, perhaps . . . you were allowed to get away with that. But when you broke a rule you knew it. You wanted to be punished—*needed* it—but the punishment did not come. That foolish leniency on the part of your parents may have been the germ of your present illness. I remind you of this, hoping you will understand that it is *entirely for your own good* that we enforce discipline. (*Looking straight at* McMURPHY.) Is there any comment? (*Silence.* McMURPHY *riffles the cards in his hands.*) Then I assume you understand me and agree. You also understand that it is *difficult* to enforce discipline in these surroundings. After all, what can we do to you? You can't be arrested. You can't be put on bread and water. You can't be sent to an institution, you're already there. All we *can* do is take away privileges. And so, after carefully considering the circumstances, we have decided to take away certain privileges which allowed—no, *encouraged* the rebellion to happen. (*Referring to her memorandum.*) First, for thirty days there will be no viewing of television. (*A groan from* SCANLON.) Second, the privilege of playing cards during recreation hours is hereby rescinded. (*The cards in* McMURPHY'S *hands go "Splat!" The* MEN'S *eyes go hopefully to him.*)

McMURPHY. (*Putting the cards away.*) 'Scuse me.

HARDING. (*Sounding sick.*) Is that all?

NURSE RATCHED. Not quite. There is one more matter we must consider. The behavior of a patient who has been here almost as long as I. Longer, I believe, than any of you. (*Smiling.*) You know, of course, to whom I refer? (*The* MEN *are puzzled at first, then turn eyes to* CHIEF BROMDEN . . . *so long a fixture, never a subject in these meetings.*) Mr. Bromden long ago was diagnosed as catatonic. The word means . . . I think you can define it, Dale?

HARDING. (*Mechanically.*) An advanced form of schizophrenia which may be marked by stupor, negativism, mutism . . .

NURSE RATCHED. Precisely. In Mr. Bromden's case marked by loss of speech and hearing. And for that reason—because it was assumed we could not communicate—we gave him up. We *forgot* poor Mr. Bromden. (*Smiles warmly at the* CHIEF *but there is apprehension gathering in his eyes and his hands grip the sides of his chair.*) That was wrong of us. But Mr. Bromden acted wrongly, too. Please don't misunderstand. We are happy to know that Mr. Bromden can be reached—but disappointed to learn he would *conceal* it from us, thereby refusing to cooperate in his own cure. And if Mr. Bromden can hear, isn't it logical to assume that he can also *speak?* I think Mr. Bromden should speak to us, don't you? His first contribution to Group Therapy. And how appropriate if those first words were an apology.

CHIEF BROMDEN. (*A whimpered plea.*) Mac . . .

NURSE RATCHED. An *apology* for the behavior that made yesterday's rebellion—

CHIEF BROMDEN. (*In terror.*) McMurphy . . . ! (NURSE RATCHED *snaps her fingers and* WARREN *comes across toward the trembling, retreating* CHIEF BROMDEN. MCMURPHY'S *foot comes out—operating independently of his will—and* WARREN *trips over it and crashes to the floor.*)

NURSE RATCHED. (*A warning.*) Mr. McMurphy—!

WARREN. (*Comes to his feet, catlike.*) Man, you *beggin'* for it!

MCMURPHY. (*Rising to block* WARREN'S *way.*) Let 'im alone.

NURSE RATCHED. Mr. McMurphy, I am *warning* you.

WARREN. (*Starts toward* CHIEF BROMDEN *once more and* MCMURPHY *swings, a powerful but clumsy round-*

house right. NURSE RATCHED *calmly signals to the Station.* NURSE FLINN *throws a switch that starts an alarm bell ringing.* WARREN *ducks lithely and sinks a fist in* MCMURPHY'S *belly that doubles him over. Joyfully, dancing about.*) Come on, you bastard, I been *waitin'* for this. Come on, stan' up an'— *Ugh!* (*Is gripped from behind and lifted high off the floor in* CHIEF BROMDEN'S *hands.* WARREN *yells in terror. BLACKOUT.*)

(*The alarm bell continues, fading as: a tight pool of light reveals the electroshock table being readied by a* TECHNICIAN *who hums as he works.* MCMURPHY, *then* BROMDEN, *are pushed roughly into the room by the* AIDES. *Both are in straitjackets.* MCMURPHY *begins to chuckle.* CHIEF BROMDEN *looks at him uncertainly.*)

MCMURPHY. (*Laughing.*) Jesus, that look on Warrens' face. That *look* when you *threw* the ol' bear hug on 'im. Aw, c'mon, Chief, why don't you laugh right out loud? You got to laugh—'specially when things ain't funny. (*Laughs again, throws a shoulder block at the* CHIEF, *stands back and gets him to retaliate.*) That's the ticket! That's the way ya keep yourself in balance. Hey, y'know something? You're gettin' bigger. Look at that foot. The size of a flatcar! You keep growin' that way and pretty soon they'll have ta spring ya. And there'll be Big Chief Bromden, cuttin' down the boulevards, men, women and kids rockin' back on their heels to peer up at 'im! "Well, well, well, what giant's this here, takin' ten feet at a step and duckin' for telephone wires? Comes stompin' through town, stops just long enough for virgins, the rest o' you twitches don't even bother linin' up!" (*His laugh rolls free, and the* CHIEF *joins him, this time more easily.* NURSE RATCHED *enters escorted by the* AIDES.)

NURSE RATCHED. (*Friendly.*) What's so amusing?

MCMURPHY. I ain't sure you'd get the point.

NURSE RATCHED. Don't you boys feel sorry for what you did?

McMURPHY. I don't guess so, ma'am. So whatever you're goin' to do, get on with it.

NURSE RATCHED. We had a meeting, Randle. The Staff agreed it might be beneficial if you were to receive shock therapy. But we won't—provided you are prepared to admit your mistakes.

McMURPHY. You got a paper I can sign?

NURSE RATCHED. A paper?

McMURPHY. Yeah, then you could add some other things. Like how I'm part of a plot to overthrow the government, and how I think life on your ward is the sweetest goddam thing this side of Hawaii, and—

NURSE RATCHED. I don't believe that would—

McMURPHY. *Then,* after I sign you bring me a blanket and a package of Red Cross cigarettes. Hooee, those Commies could of learned a few things from you, lady!

NURSE RATCHED. Randle, we are trying to help you.

McMURPHY. Do I get my pants slit? You gonna shave my head? (NURSE RATCHED *turns from him, nods her head abruptly to the* TECHNICIAN, *and exits.* CHIEF BROMDEN *whimpers as the* AIDES *grab* McMURPHY *and strap him to the table.*) Don't be scared, Chief. I'll go first. If they can't hurt me, they can't hurt you. (*The* TECHNICIAN *smears a compound on his temples.*) What's that?

TECHNICIAN. Conductant.

McMURPHY. Anointest my head with conductant! Do I get a crown of thorns?

CHIEF BROMDEN. (*Whimpering.*) Papa. Papa.

McMURPHY. Don't holler, Chief. Or if you *got* to holler, make it "Guts ball."

CHIEF BROMDEN. (*Trembling.*) Guts ball.

McMURPHY. Atta Injun! (*The* TECHNICIAN *presses a silver band over his forehead.*) Hoo boy, I *do* get a crown.

CHIEF BROMDEN. (*Trembling.*) Guts ball.

McMurphy. (*Singing.*)
"Get Wildroot Cream Oil, Cholly,
Helps keep your hair in trim . . . !"

(*The* Technician *jams a rubber mouthpiece between his teeth.*)

Chief Bromden. Guts ball. Guts ball.

McMurphy. (*Through mouthpiece.*)
"It's non-alcoholic—Cholly—
Mathe with thoothin' lanolin . . ."

Technician. (*Taking up wires with contacts from shock machine.*) Hold him! (*The* Aides *fling themselves across* McMurphy's *body.*)

Chief Bromden. (*As the* Technician *touches the wires to the band around* McMurphy's *head.*) Guts *BALL-L-L!* (*A blaze of white light.* McMurphy's *body snaps into a rigid arc. SOUND: An electronic scream with voices within it shouting, "Air raid, air raid . . . !" The lights DIM OUT. The sound fades, cross-blending into:*)

Children's Voices. (*On tape; singsonging.*)
Intra, mintra, cute-ra corn,
Apple seed and apple thorn,
Wire, brier, limber lock,
Three geese in a flock.
One flew east,
One flew west,
And one flew over the cuckoo's nest . . . !

(*Their laughter rises; then fades. LIGHTS TO FULL on the Day Room.* Harding, Martini, Billy, Cheswick *and* Scanlon *are there, and* Ruckly *in his usual position. The* Men *are mumbling intensely among themselves. They break off as* Nurse Ratched *and* Dr. Spivey *enter, moving briskly.*)

Nurse Ratched. (*Without preamble.*) May I,

Doctor! (DOCTOR *waves consent.*) Gentlemen, we have just come from the Treasurer's office, and we have here a memorandum of extreme interest. It concerns Patient Randle McMurphy.

SCANLON. (*Truculently.*) Yeah, where you got 'im? Up in Disturbed?

NURSE RATCHED. No, Mr. Scanlon, he is in the Recovery Room and will be back very shortly. (*Silence, and she smiles around the room, holding up the memorandum.*) This, gentlemen, is a record of Mr. McMurphy's gains in the short time he has been croupier of his little Monte Carlo here on the ward. How much did you lose, Billy? Mr. Harding? I think you all have some idea of what your personal losses were, but do you know what Mr. McMurphy's winnings come to? Acording to deposits he has made, over three hundred dollars. (BILLY *whistles.*) I just thought it would be better if there were no delusions about his motives.

HARDING. (*Stirring.*) Miss Ratched . . . he never made any *pretense* about his motives.

CHESWICK. That's right!

SCANLON. *Said* he was out to take us and by God he done it!

CHESWICK. (*Who can see the Ward entrance.*) Mac! (MCMURPHY *and* BROMDEN *are pushed into the room by the* AIDES. *Both stand slackbodied as though they'd been wiped out by the EST. Then* MCMURPHY *snaps out of the shamming.*)

MCMURPHY. Stand back, you peckerheads, here comes the champ! Ol' McMurphy, the ten-thousand-watt psychopath! Howdy, buddies! Howdy, Doc! (*With a bow.*) Miss Rat-shit. (*Takes* BROMDEN *and makes him stand on the rocking chair; jumps to the bench.*) And here, ladeez and gennulmun, right here in front of your eyes, the Wild Man who dotes on high voltage and eats three aides for breakfast each and every morning! (*Playfully roars at the* CHIEF *who weakly echoes the roar. Not satisfied,* MCMURPHY *roars back until the* CHIEF *responds with a full-bodied roar.*)

NURSE RATCHED. Mr. McMurphy. We are in the middle of a meeting.

MCMURPHY. Oh, *do* continue. (*Rubbing his hands eagerly.*) Who we tearin' up today?

NURSE RATCHED. Since you found it so enjoyable, perhaps a few more treatments . . . ?

MCMURPHY. Oh, please, ma'am, *yes*. Look at the good a few measly volts have done me. (*Advancing, "dialing" her breasts.*) I bet if we doubled the charge, I could pick up Channel Eight!

NURSE RATCHED. Doctor.

DR. SPIVEY. Yes, Miss Ratched?

NURSE RATCHED. I'd like to withdraw that suggestion as to further shock.

MCMURPHY. (*Reproachfully.*) Oh-h!

NURSE RATCHED. Yes . . . I think it might be wise to consider . . . surgical procedure.

MCMURPHY. Ma'am?

NURSE RATCHED. An operation. Quite simple, really. We've had an excellent record in aggressive cases.

MCMURPHY. Aggressive? Why, ma'am, I'm friendly as a pup. There's no cause to do any cuttin'.

NURSE RATCHED. (*Smiling, friendly.*) Randle, there's no *cutting* involved. We simply—

MCMURPHY. Besides, it wouldn't do no good to lop 'em off. I got another pair at home. Big as baseballs!

DR. SPIVEY. Haw! (*And the* MEN *laugh, too.* DR. SPIVEY *turns to leave.*)

NURSE RATCHED. (*Smile frozen.*) One moment, Doctor. I should like to return to the subject.

DR. SPIVEY. What subject?

NURSE RATCHED. The question of surgical procedure for Patient McMurphy.

DR. SPIVEY. (*Shaking his head.*) Not warranted except in cases of uncontrollable violence.

NURSE RATCHED. He has exhibited violence.

DR. SPIVEY. Shall we say there was a certain . . . provocation? (*With unexpected firmness.*) No, Miss Ratched. Since you have brought up the matter in Group rather than Staff, I shall state my opinion. I do not approve surgical procedure in the absence of recurrent violence.

NURSE RATCHED. (*Tightly.*) And if it *should* recur?

DR. SPIVEY. Then . . . we may reconsider. Mr. McMurphy—I would bear that in mind. (*Exits.*)

NURSE RATCHED. (*Smiling brightly.*) Behave yourself, boys. (*Exits, followed by the* AIDES.)

MCMURPHY. (*Shouting after her.*) *Do* change your mind about those treatments, ma'am, I just *adore* your little battery charger! (*His face changes when she is gone. To* HARDING.) What was that stuff about "surgical procedure?"

HARDING. I guess she means lobotomy.

MCMURPHY. What's that?

HARDING. Well, you might call it a sort of . . . castration of the brain.

MCMURPHY. Okay, okay, what's it *do* to you?

HARDING. (*Gestures to* MCMURPHY *to follow him, and crosses to stand before* RUCKLY.) They say he used to be a real rough character.

MCMURPHY. (*Gazing at* RUCKLY . . . *the slack body, empty eyes. Softly:*) Jee-zuss . . .

HARDING. (*Impulsively.*) Mac, we've been talking it over, the boys and I. We think you ought to get out of here.

MCMURPHY. (*His eyes still on* RUCKLY.) Get out of here?

CHESWICK. (*Eagerly.*) That's right, we figured out a way. Soon's it gets dark tonight, I set fire to my mattress. Then we make a holler, and when the firemen come they're going to leave the door open, aren't they? Then we rush you out!

MCMURPHY. (*Turns to them, grinning.*) Boys, it's as good as a TV show, and I thank you. But if I went I'd miss the party.

CHESWICK. Party?

MCMURPHY. You forgotten?

SCANLON. Holy cow!

MCMURPHY. You wouldn't want me to miss Billy cashin' in his virginity?

HARDING. But, Mac—

MCMURPHY. Don't worry, boys, them windows will be open tonight. So I can sashay right on out. We make it a goin'-away party, huh? (*Sees* WARREN *entering.*) Woops, cool it.

WARREN. Supper time, gennelmen, move yo' feet. (*He goes to pull the "nails" from* RUCKLY'S *hands and the* ACUTES *follow them out.*)

MCMURPHY. (*Catching* BILLY'S *attention.*) Psst. (BILLY *comes to him and they are alone. Confidentially:*) You take your vitamins, Billy? 'Cause I'm warnin' you, that Candy girl . . . !

BILLY. Aw, Mac . . .

MCMURPHY. Now, don't go bashful on me, I'm bettin' five bucks you burn that woman down!

BILLY. That's right . . . that's what I'm gonna do . . . (*Squirming pleasurably.*) I'm goin' to . . . b-burn her down!

MCMURPHY. Hey, you got any bread?

BILLY. How much?

MCMURPHY. 'Bout fifty bucks?

BILLY. Fifty—! (*Resentfully.*) What for?

MCMURPHY. Candy's layin' out for liquor. And there's old Turkle to take care of, and . . . why the hell you lookin' down your nose like that?

BILLY. Something Miss R-Ratched said.

MCMURPHY. What'd she say?

BILLY. How you were always coming out ahead. Always *w-winning* things. (*Turns from* MCMURPHY *and exits.*)

MCMURPHY. Winning. (*His eyes close, his body sags and his hands come up to where the electrodes were . . . his face abruptly haggard and defenseless.*) Hoo boy. *Winning.* (*He exits, feet dragging.*)

(*LIGHTS DIM to Night Lighting.* AIDE TURKLE *enters the deserted room from the outer corridor. After making sure that he's alone he sits, lights up a marijuana joint and takes a deep drag.* CHESWICK *comes creeping out of the dorm.*)

CHESWICK. Sssssssssssst!

TURKLE. (*Startled, turns his flashlight on* CHESWICK'S *face.*) Lord he'p me, I thought you was a snake!

CHESWICK. (*An excited whisper.*) She showed up yet?

TURKLE. She who?

CHESWICK. Candy!

TURKLE. (*Blandly.*) I don't know nothin' 'bout no candy.

CHESWICK. (*Dismayed.*) Mac said he made a deal with you.

TURKLE. I ain't got the slightest inclination what you talkin' 'bout.

CHESWICK. Don't go away! (*Disappears back into the dormitory.*)

TURKLE. (*Exhaling smoke.*) I ain't goin' nowhere. (MCMURPHY *emerges with* CHESWICK *at his shoulder.*)

MCMURPHY. Turkey, ol' boy! What's the beef?

TURKLE. Ain't no beef.

MCMURPHY. So?

TURKLE. Ain't no money changed hands, neither.

MCMURPHY. (*Digs in his pocket for a wad of bills.*) There y'are. Begged, borrowed and stole.

TURKLE. (*Taking it, mournfully.*) You know, they fin' out 'bout this they fire my ass.

MCMURPHY. She's bringin' liquor, Turkey.

TURKLE. (*Brightening.*) Yeah?

MCMURPHY. Bottle of Scotch and one of vodka. Which d'you want?

TURKLE. (*Deliberating.*) Sorta like 'em both.

MCMURPHY. Hey, what're we supposed to drink?

TURKLE. (*Morally.*) You ain't supposed to drink at *all.*

MCMURPHY. (*To* CHESWICK, *who is at the window.*) Any sign?

CHESWICK. Nary sign.

MCMURPHY. (*Slaps his forehead.*) Hoo boy, am I stupid! How they gonna find the right window in the dark? (*To* TURKLE.) Turn on the lights.

TURKLE. Hey, now, tha's *dangerous.* Miz Ratched, she see the ward lit up—

MCMURPHY. Come on, Turkey, she's asleep.

TURKLE. (*Grumbling as he finds the key.*) That ol' shitpoke *never* sleep. (*The LIGHTS GO ON and* HARDING *and the* OTHER ACUTES *come piling out of the dormitory.*)

MARTINI. (*Racing in.*) Hey, where's the party?

MCMURPHY. (*Indicating the latrine.*) In there.

MARTINI. (*Joyously.*) Oh, boy! (*He races into the latrine.*)

MCMURPHY. (*To* TURKLE.) Gimme the window key.

TURKLE. I ain't s'pose to let these keys off'n—

MCMURPHY. *Gimme.*

TURKLE. (*Muttering as he removes it from the ring.*) Tha' better be *good* liquor.

MCMURPHY. (*Tossing the key to* HARDING.) Open the window, huh?

HARDING. (*At the window.*) Sssssssss! She walks in beauty!

MCMURPHY. Well, let 'er in! Let this mad stud at her!

BILLY. (*As* HARDING *unlocks the screen.*) Look, McM-M-Murphy, wait—

MCMURPHY. Don't you mama-murphy me, Billy Boy, it's too late to back out now. (CANDY *is climbing through the window, helped by* HARDING *and* SCANLON, *impeded by the bottles she carried in each hand. She's quite tipsy.*)

CANDY. (*Charging at* MCMURPHY.) You damned

McMurphy! (*She flings her arms about him to kiss him, and* TURKLE *adroitly snatches the bottle of Scotch.*) Hey, what the hell—!

McMURPHY. That's okay, baby. (*Inspecting the half-empty bottle of vodka.*) What happened to this one?

CANDY. (*Giggling, patting her stomach.*) We got the rest of it right here.

McMURPHY. We?

CANDY. Oh, lordy, I forgot, Sandra's out there!

SANDRA. (*Is struggling through the window with* HARDING'S *help, showing a lot of leg.*) Hiya, Mac.

McMURPHY. Sandy, baby! (McMURPHY *kisses her.* SANDRA *is a big, earthy wench. Like* CANDY, *she is drunk.*) What'd you do with your husband?

SANDRA. (*As* HARDING *closes the screen and pockets the key.*) That creep!

CANDY. (*Giggling.*) She up and left him. Ain't that a gasser?

SANDRA. Lissen, you can take just so many funsies like worms in your cold cream and frogs down your bra. Cheesus, what a creep!

CANDY. (*With warmth.*) Hello, Billy!

BILLY. (*Bashfully.*) Hello, C-C-C-C—

CANDY. Never mind. (*She kisses him, then pulls him to a chair and sits on his lap.*)

SANDRA. (*Suddenly.*) *Ouch!*

McMURPHY. Ya okay, baby?

SANDRA. (*Darkly, eyeing* SCANLON.) Somebody pinched my ass.

McMURPHY. I gotta find somethin' for us to drink! Cheswick, get me somethin' to mix it in. (*Takes the keys and opens the Nurses' Station.* MARTINI *and* SCANLON *follow.* SANDRA *goes circling, looking over the* MEN.)

SANDRA. Whooee, Candy girl, is this for real? I mean, are we in an *asylum?* (*To* HARDING.) Tell the truth, are you really nuts?

HARDING. Absolutely, madam. We are psycho-ceramics, the cracked pots of humanity. Would you like me to decipher a Rorschach? (CHESWICK *rolls in an enema bag with tube attached, on a stand.*)

CHESWICK. Cocktail shaker!

MCMURPHY. (*On microphone.*) Medication! (*Comes out of Station laden with jugs and bottles of medicine.*)

HARDING. (*Reading the label on a bottle of cherry-colored liquid.*) Artificial coloring, citric acid. Sixty percent inert materials.

MCMURPHY. (*Pointing out a line.*) Twenty-two per-cent alcohol. (*Is pouring liquids into the bag.*)

HARDING. (*Reading the next label.*) Ten percent codeine. Warning: May Be Habit Forming.

MCMURPHY. (*Seizing it.*) Nothin' like a good bad habit.

HARDING. (*Next bottle.*) Tincture of nux vomica.

MCMURPHY. (*Emptying it in.*) That'll give it body.

CHESWICK. (*Returning from the Station.*) Here's some cups.

MCMURPHY. (*Shakes up the cocktail with professional dexterity. Tastes it. Clicks his teeth together loudly.*) If we cut it a *leetle* bit . . . (*Pours the remaining vodka into the shaker and squeezes it.*)

SANDRA. (*Giggling.*) Jeez, what a shindy. Is this really happening?

HARDING. No, ma'am. The whole thing is a collaboration between Franz Kafka and Mark Twain.

MCMURPHY. (*Pouring.*) Bar's open!

HARDING. (*Tasting.*) Dee-licious!

CANDY. (*Taking a sip.*) Tastes like cough medicine.

SANDRA. (*Getting to her feet.*) 'Scuse me, I gotta tinkle. (*She goes, weaving.*)

HARDING. You know this stuff gives one the feeling of—of—

MCMURPHY. (*Grinning.*) No more rabbits?

HARDING. Old friend, you have taught me that mental illness can have the aspect of power. Perhaps the more insane a man is the more powerful he can become.

SCANLON. Sure— Hitler! (*There is a scream, and* SANDRA *comes running from the dormitory with* RUCKLY *in pursuit.*)

RUCKLY. F-f-fuck 'em all!

SANDRA. This damn place is dangerous!

CHESWICK. (*Leads her to the latrine.*) Went the wrong way, lady. (MARTINI *is in the Station, fiddling with the tape machine. Now it comes on: MUSIC.*)

CANDY. C'mon, Billy! (*Pulls him to his feet and they dance, cheek to cheek. The* MEN *fall back from them as they hold each other closely, moving more slowly . . . and they are looking into each other's eyes.*)

MCMURPHY. (*Dangling* TURKLE'S *keys.*) How about the Seclusion Room?

CHESWICK. (*Happily.*) Sure, the place is one big mattress!

HARDING. One moment! Shall we send them off without benefit of ceremony? Come, children—here, before me. (*Mounts a chair as* BILLY *and* CANDY *link hands before him and the* GROUP *forms up in rough semblance of a wedding.*) Mac, would you bring Ruckly? We can use him as a centerpiece. (MCMURPHY *brings* RUCKLY, *arranges him in his crucifixion pose.*) Dearly beloved, we are gathered in the sight of Freud to celebrate the end of innocence and cheer on its demise. Who stands sponsor for the benedict?

MCMURPHY. (*Moving to* BILLY'S *side.*) R. P. McMurphy.

HARDING. And for the bride?

SANDRA. (*Coming to* CANDY'S *side.*) Me!

HARDING. Very well, then. Do you, Candy Starr, take this man to love and cherish for such brief time as rules and regulations may allow?

CANDY. I do.

HARDING. Do you, Billy Bibbit, take this woman to have and hold until the night shift changes and our revels end?

BILLY. I duh-duh-duh—I duh—

MCMURPHY. He does!

HARDING. Most merciful God, we ask that You accept these two into Your kingdom with Your well-known compassion. And keep the door ajar for all the rest of us . . . for this may be our final fling and we are doomed, henceforth, to the terrible burden of sanity. As comes the dawn we shall most assuredly be lined up against the wall and fired upon with bullets of Miltown! Librium! Thorazine! Go, my children—sin while ye may, for tomorrow we shall be tranquilized. (CANDY *and* BILLY *kiss. They exit to singing of the Wedding March, under an arch formed by* CHESWICK *and* SCANLON'S *arms.*)

MCMURPHY. (*Putting down* RUCKLY'S *arms.*) Mr. Ruckly, you did a fine job. (SANDRA *sits on the floor, sniffling.*) Sandra, baby!

SANDRA. Well, it was so damn beautiful. (MCMURPHY *hugs her.*)

HARDING. (*With a sigh.*) Mac, we're sure going to miss you.

MCMURPHY. So why don't you all come along?

HARDING. Oh, I'll be going soon. But I've got to do it my own way. Sign the papers. Call my wife and say, "Pick me up at a certain time." You understand?

MCMURPHY. Sure, but . . . what is it with you guys?

HARDING. You mean what drove us here in the first place? Oh, I don't know . . . a lot of theories . . . but I do know what drives people like you—strong people—crazy.

MCMURPHY. Okay, what?

HARDING. People like us.

HCMURPHY. (*Uncertainly.*) Bull.

HARDING. Oh, yes, my friend.

McMurphy. Hey, what's happening to the party? Drink up, you mother-lovin' loonies, this is Big Mac tendin' bar, and when he pours let no man—! (Chief Bromden, *having taken several belts from the bottle, lets out a wild whoop, startling* Everyone.) Chief, was that you?

Chief Bromden. (*Equally startled.*) I guess so.

McMurphy. What ya doin', declarin' war?

Chief Bromden. My tribe never made war on nobody.

Turkle. That was a sorry damn tribe. (Turkle *flinches as* Chief Bromden *moves toward him.*)

Chief Bromden. Maybe that was our mistake. We should of! (*He whoops again, pleased with the sound, then goes into a shuffling war dance, accompanying himself with chanted Indian gutturals. The* Others *fall delightedly into line and it becomes a snake-dance, weaving its noisy way around the room.* Nurse Ratched *enters from the corridor and stands frozen in incredulity. She is there some moments before anyone becomes aware.*)

McMurphy. Hiya, kid! We got room for one more. (Nurse Ratched *flees.* Harding *drops out of the dance.*)

Harding. (*Yelling.*) Stop! Quiet! Shut *up*, everybody. (*With delayed horror.*) Was that . . . did I see . . . ?

McMurphy. (*Aggrieved.*) I assed her to stay.

Harding. Oh, God, she went to get help. (*Hurrying to the window.*) Mac, you've got to get out of here.

McMurphy. (*Cheerfully tipsy.*) Okay, soon's I say g'bye to my buddies.

Harding. (*Swinging open the grille.*) In a *hurry*.

Turkle. I don't know 'bout him—but I am goin' to drag ass! (*Climbs onto the sill, tumbles out of sight.*)

Harding. Sandy!

Sandra. You coming, Mac?

McMURPHY. (*Shaking hands with the* MEN.) Best damned buddies I ever had!

HARDING. (*As* SANDRA *climbs through the window.*) Don't hang *around . . . !*

McMURPHY. (*To* BROMDEN.) You gonna be all right? 'Cause if you ain't I'll hear about it, and I'll come bustin' back inta this place . . . !

HARDING. (*Crossing to him.*) Come *on*, Mac.

McMURPHY. Okay, all *right.* (WARREN *and* WILLIAMS *not quite fully dressed, come in fast.* NURSE RATCHED *is close behind.*)

NURSE RATCHED. (*Snapping it.*) Stand still, everyone. Just remain right where you are. (*Switches on full lights. The* MEN *blink confusedly.*) Warren. Room check. (WARREN *races off.*) Williams—get this place in order. (*Strolling about, easily.*) So we've had a party. Thrown, no doubt, by Mr. McMurphy? (*To* McMURPHY.) I wonder . . . was there some sort of profit in it?

McMURPHY. (*Scornfully.*) Oh, very smart. Tryin' to bug me till I blow my top. Well, shove it, sister, 'cause I'm hip. And I am *leavin'* . . . (WARREN *pushes* BILLY *and* CANDY *onstage. They are disheveled and confused, covering their eyes against the light.* McMURPHY *stops dead at the window.*)

NURSE RATCHED. Where were they?

WARREN. (*Grinning.*) Seclusion Room. On the floor.

NURSE RATCHED. William—Bibbit. Oh, Billy, I'm so ashamed!

BILLY. (*Considers.*) I'm not.

McMURPHY. Thassit, Billy—! (*The* OTHERS *erupt into cheers.*)

NURSE RATCHED. You be silent! Oh, Billy . . . a woman like *this.*

BILLY. Like what?

NURSE RATCHED. A cheap—low—painted—

BILLY. She is not! She's good, and sweet, and—!

ALL. Attaboy, Billy!

NURSE RATCHED. (*Dragging* CANDY *forward.*) *Look* at her.

CANDY. (*Fleeing to* McMURPHY.) Mac—!

BILLY. (*Simultaneously.*) You leave her alone!

NURSE RATCHED. (*Changing tactics.*) Billy, have you thought how your poor mother is going to take this? She's always been so proud of your decency. You know what this is going to do to her. You know, don't you?

BILLY. No. No. You don't nuh-need—

NURSE RATCHED. Don't need to tell her? How could I not?

BILLY. (*Beginning to crumble.*) Duh—duh—don't tell her, Miss Ratched. Duh-duh—

NURSE RATCHED. Billy, dear, I have to. I have to tell her that you were found on the floor of the Seclusion Room . . . with this . . . prostitute. That you and she—

BILLY. No! I d-d-didn't! I mean, she m-made me do it!

NURSE RATCHED. I can't believe she pulled you in there forcibly.

BILLY. (*Wildly.*) It was the others. They m-made fun of me. Thuh-they—

NURSE RATCHED. Who, Billy?

BILLY. All of them. Thuh-thuh—they teased me. They c-c-called me names.

NURSE RATCHED. Who, Billy?

BILLY. (*Clutching her knees, sobbing.*) McMuh-Murphy. It was McMurphy . . .

McMURPHY. (*In dismay.*) Billy . . .

NURSE RATCHED. All right, Billy. No one will hurt you. I want you to go to Dr. Spivey's office. Wait for him there, you'll be needing attention.

BILLY. Miss Ratched, you're not going to tell my mother?

NURSE RATCHED. It's all right, Billy, it's going to be all right.

BILLY. (*Catching* McMURPHY'S *gaze.*) McMurphy . . . ! (*Breaks and runs, out the Ward door.* WARREN *follows.*)

NURSE RATCHED. (*To* CANDY; *hard.*) And you, miss, if you're not out of here within ten seconds I will have you jailed as the common prostitute you are.

CANDY. You coming, Mac? (*She flees through the window.*)

NURSE RATCHED. (*To* MCMURPHY.) Aren't you? There's no reason to stay, you've already plundered these poor, sick people of everything they had. So run, Mr. McMurphy. Save your own skin while the saving is—

WARREN. (*Off; yelling frantically.*) Nurse Ratched! Oh, my God, Nurse Ratched, quick . . . ! (NURSE RATCHED *hurries out, followed by* WILLIAMS.)

HARDING. (*After a silence.*) Nobody's blaming you, Mac.

SCANLON. (*Unconvincingly.*) That's right. Nobody's blamin' you. (MCMURPHY *looks at them one by one, and their eyes won't meet his. He sits, slowly, waiting for what is to come.* NURSE RATCHED *enters, the* AIDES *following. She crosses directly to* MCMURPHY.)

NURSE RATCHED. He cut his throat. (MCMURPHY *does not look up.*) He went into the Doctor's desk and he found an instrument and he cut his throat. That poor boy has killed himself. He is in there now, in the Doctor's chair, with his throat cut. (MCMURPHY *doesn't move or answer.*) I hope you're satisfied. Playing with human lives. Gambling with human lives as though you were God. Are you God, Mr. McMurphy? Somehow I don't think you are God. (*She turns her back and crosses toward the Station.* MCMURPHY *sighs deeply and heaves himself to his feet.*)

HARDING. (*Seeing his intention; blocking him.*) No, Mac, it's what she wants!

MCMURPHY. (*In helpless fury, knocking* HARDING *aside.*) *Don'tcha think I know it?*

NURSE RATCHED. (*Signaling the* AIDES *not to interfere; smiling as* MCMURPHY *walks toward her.*) Come on, Mr. McMurphy. Come on . . . (*He reaches out and rips her uniform open down the front. Her knee comes up viciously, and* McMURPHY *barely eludes it.* NURSE RATCHED *screams, the scream cut off as his hands lock about her throat. The cry is caught up and continued in* CHIEF BROMDEN'S *throat as he spins away. A single light stabs down at him as all other lights BLACK OUT. There is a hissing sound, then the thudding of the Black Machine with electronic counterpoint.*)

CHIEF BROMDEN. (*Voice on tape.*) Papa, they got to me again. Some way they got the wires on me and they're givin' orders. Go right. Go left. Do this. Do that. Sign the papers twenty times and don't step on the grass. Where can I run? How can I get away? Papa, there's no place to hide no more. No place to hide! (*LIGHTS UP on the Day Room. It is post-supper.* CHIEF BROMDEN *is hunched in catatonic stance.* HARDING *is at the card table dealing blackjack to* CHESWICK, SCANLON *and* MARTINI.)

HARDING. (*Imitating* McMURPHY'S *style.*) Hey-a, hey-a, come on, suckers, the game is twenty-one, you hit or you sit. What do you do, Scanlon?

SCANLON. I wasn't payin' any mind.

HARDING. Well, pay some mind.

SCANLON. (*Getting up restlessly.*) Gosh, if we only *knew*. Where they got him. What they're doin'. Damn near a whole *week* now.

CHESWICK. Hey, you know what a guy down at the dining room told me? He says McMurphy knocked out two aides and took their keys away from them and escaped!

SCANLON. (*Hopefully.*) That *sounds* like Mac.

HARDING. What ward was your informant from?

CHESWICK. Disturbed.

MARTINI. Somebody told me they'd caught him and sent him back to the Work Farm.

HARDING. Who?

MARTINI. (*Looking around.*) Somebody . . . !

HARDING. (*Wearily.*) And a loony down in Occupational Therapy told me that McMurphy had sprouted wings and was last seen soaring in lazy circles overhead, defecating on the hospital.

MARTINI. (*Open-mouthed.*) Honest?

(HARDING *throws up his hands in disgust.* WARREN *enters, harbinger for* NURSE RATCHED, *who is close behind.* NURSE RATCHED *wears a bandage around her throat. Her manner has changed; warier, and her eyes are nervous.* WILLIAMS *appears in the doorway, waiting.*)

NURSE RATCHED. (*Her voice husky.*) Isn't it past your bedtime?

CHESWICK. (*Advancing.*) Miss Ratched— (NURSE RATCHED *takes a step backward.*) —what we want to know—

HARDING. Is McMurphy coming back? I think we have a right—

NURSE RATCHED. I agree, Mr. Harding. He will be back. (*There is hostile skepticism.*) Don't you believe me?

HARDING. (*Deliberately.*) Lady, we think you are full of bull.

NURSE RATCHED. (*A pause, calmly.*) I assure you, McMurphy will be back. Now I think it's time you were in bed? (*She faces them steadily; and the* MEN *file silently into the dormitory. Only* CHIEF BROMDEN, *unnoticed and unmoving, remains. To* WARREN.) Bring him in. (WARREN *and* WILLIAMS *wheel in a gurney bed upon which* MCMURPHY *lies covered by a blanket. He is immobile but for minor twitching. There are great purplish bruises about his eyes, and a thin line of spittle runs from his mouth. Following* NURSE RATCHED'S *signals the* AIDES *position the bed.*) That's fine, boys. (*The* AIDES *exit silently on their rubber shoes.* NURSE RATCHED *feels* MCMURPHY'S *pulse, straightens the blanket. Softly, looking down at him:*) That's just fine. (*She exits.*)

(CHIEF BROMDEN *turns his head, crosses slowly to the bed, stands there studying the* FIGURE. *From the dormitory* CHESWICK *enters. Then,* SCANLON *and* MARTINI. *They arrange themselves about the bed, not too close.* CHESWICK, *at the foot, lifts the chart that hangs there and holds it to the feeble light.*)

SCANLON. What's it say?

CHESWICK. McMurphy, Randle Patrick. Postoperative. Pre-frontal lobotomy.

SCANLON. So they done it to 'im.

CHIEF BROMDEN. (*Voice low and harsh.*) That ain't McMurphy.

SCANLON. (*Surprised.*) No?

CHIEF BROMDEN. Some dummy they rigged up.

CHESWICK. (*Startled.*) You think so?

CHIEF BROMDEN. Factory-made.

MARTINI. Hey, I bet he's right!

SCANLON. Sure! What're they trying to put over on us?

CHESWICK. (*Dubiously.*) They did a pretty fair job, though. See? The busted nose. Even the sideburns.

MARTINI. Look, its eyes is open!

SCANLON. (*As they bend over, peering.*) All smoked up.

CHESWICK. Nobody inside.

CHIEF BROMDEN. Eyes. Couple a burnt-out fuses.

SCANLON. How stupid does that ol' bitch think we are? (CHIEF BROMDEN *slides a pillow out from under* MCMURPHY'S *head.*)

MARTINI. Whatcha doin', Chief?

CHIEF BROMDEN. You think Mac would want this thing sittin' around the Day Room twenty-thirty years with his name stuck on it?

MARTINI. (*Wistfully, as with tacit unanimity the*

MEN *turn away from the* CHIEF, *ignoring what he is doing.*) Gee, I wish McMurphy would come back.

CHESWICK. (*Brightly.*) Hey, you remember that time he pinched Miss Ratched on the butt and said he was just trying to stay in contact?

SCANLON. (*Chortling.*) And them things he'd write in the Log Book? "Madam, do you wear a B cup or a C cup or any old cup at all?" (*The laughter becomes general.* CHIEF BROMDEN *is pressing the pillow down on* MCMURPHY'S *face.* MCMURPHY'S *body jerks and thrashes, fighting with indomitable vitality.*)

CHESWICK. And that time in the dining room when he flipped a piece of butter on the wall and bet it would reach the floor by seven-thirty?

MARTINI. And he *won!* (*The glee rises higher.*)

CHESWICK. D'you remember the time that little nurse—

SCANLON. The one that wears a cross!

CHESWICK. —she dropped a pill down the front of her uniform and McMurphy tries to help her get it out, and she hollers—

SCANLON. (*Falsetto.*) "Rape! Rape! Rape!" (*They are whooping with laughter as* HARDING *enters from the dormitory, wearing pajamas and a robe.*)

HARDING. What in the hell is going on? You guys are supposed to be . . . to be in . . . . (*He becomes aware of what is happening. Horrified.*) Chief! (*He flings himself on* BROMDEN.) Chief, let go. (*The* MEN *move towards the gurney.*) Chief . . . let go. Let . . . go. (*Pulls with all his strength.* CHIEF BROMDEN *stumbles away. Flings aside the pillow. Feels for pulse in* MCMURPHY'S *neck. In soft horror:*) Oh, Christ Jesus . . . (*The* CHIEF *begins to cry.* HARDING *turns from him and races to the window.*)

CHESWICK. (*Curiously.*) What're you doing?

HARDING. I've still got the key! (*He unlocks the grille, swings it open.*) All right, Chief. Get going. Chief, do you hear me?

SCANLON. Why you hollerin' at him?

HARDING. If he's gone they can't prove anything!

MARTINI. He didn't do nothin' wrong!

CHESWICK. Anybody can die, postoperative. Happens all the time.

SCANLON. *We'll* never tell.

HARDING. I know. But he *will*.

CHIEF BROMDEN. (*It penetrates. Quaveringly.*) What should I do?

HARDING. Beat it!

CHIEF BROMDEN. Out . . . there?

HARDING. Flag a ride on the highway. Head north, up into Canada.

CHESWICK. That's right, Chief, they never go after AWOL's.

SCANLON. And we'll say he was alive *after* you busted out.

CHIEF BROMDEN. I'm afraid.

HARDING. Chief—

CHIEF BROMDEN. I can't do it, I'm not big enough!

HARDING. You're as big as you're going to get!

CHIEF BROMDEN. No. No. McMurphy said . . . he says . . . (*He moves toward the panel at the foot of the Station.*)

HARDING. (*A wail.*) Chief, what are you *doing?*

CHIEF BROMDEN. (*Knocking* HARDING *aside.*) McMurphy said . . . (*He crosses to the panel, heaves upward on it. Nothing happens. He takes a deep breath, tries again. There comes a cracking sound, a screech and ripping as the panel pulls loose. Electrical cables snap; there is the blue-white blaze and the ripping sound of short-circuits. The nightlights and the lights in the Station go out. An alarm bell sets up a distant clamor.*)

HARDING. Oh, Christ, they'll come down with an army! (*He pushes* BROMDEN *toward the window.*)

CHIEF BROMDEN. I done it. (*Exulting.*) I done it, Harding. I'm full size again!

HARDING. Okay, Chief, *go.* (*Gripping his hand.*) You're going to make it out there.

CHIEF BROMDEN. Yeah . . . (*Smiles at the world outside.*) I been away a long, long time . . .

(*MUSIC FADES IN—instrumental "My Horses Ain't Hungry"—as:* BROMDEN *slides lightly through the window and is gone.* HARDING *closes the grille, drops the key outside. The* MEN *cluster at the window, seeing* BROMDEN *off. The single shaft of light on* MCMURPHY'S *body, and all other lights, DIM SLOWLY TO OUT.*)

THE END

Other Publications for Your Interest

A WEEKEND NEAR MADISON

(LITTLE THEATRE—COMIC DRAMA)

By KATHLEEN TOLAN

2 men, 3 women—Interior

This recent hit from the famed Actors Theatre of Louisville, a terrific ensemble play about male-female relationships in the 80's, was praised by *Newsweek* as "warm, vital, glowing . . . full of wise ironies and unsentimental hopes". The story concerns a weekend reunion of old college friends now in their early thirties. The occasion is the visit of Vanessa, the queen bee of the group, who is now the leader of a lesbian/feminist rock band. Vanessa arrives at the home of an old friend who is now a psychiatrist hand in hand with her naif-like lover, who also plays in the band. Also on hand are the psychiatrist's wife, a novelist suffering from writer's block; and his brother, who was once Vanessa's lover and who still loves her. In the course of the weekend, Vanessa reveals that she and her lover desperately want to have a child—and she tries to persuade her former male lover to father it, not understanding that he might have some feelings about the whole thing. *Time Magazine* heard "the unmistakable cry of an infant hit . . . Playwright Tolan's work radiates promise and achievement."

(#25051)

PASTORALE

(LITTLE THEATRE—COMEDY)

By DEBORAH EISENBERG

3 men, 4 women—Interior
(plus 1 or 2 bit parts and 3 optional extras)

"Deborah Eisenberg is one of the freshest and funniest voices in some seasons."—Newsweek. Somewhere out in the country Melanie has rented a house and in the living room she, her friend Rachel who came for a weekend but forgets to leave, and their school friend Steve (all in their mid-20s) spend nearly a year meandering through a mental landscape including such concerns as phobias, friendship, work, sex, slovenliness and epistemology. Other people happen by: Steve's young girlfriend Celia, the virtuous and annoying Edie, a man who Melanie has picked up in a bar, and a couple who appear during an intense conversation and observe the sofa is on fire. The lives of the three friends inevitably proceed and eventually draw them, the better prepared perhaps by their months on the sofa, in separate directions. "The most original, funniest new comic voice to be heard in New York theater since Beth Henley's 'Crimes of the Heart.'"—N.Y. Times. "A very funny, stylish comedy."—The New Yorker. "Wacky charm and wayward wit."—New York Magazine. "Delightful."—N.Y. Post. "Uproarious . . . the play is a world unto itself, and it spins."—N.Y. Sunday Times.

(#18016)

A Man for All Seasons

By ROBERT BOLT

DRAMA—2 ACTS—11 men, 3 women—Unit set

Garlands of awards and critical praise greeted this long-run success in both New York and London. In both productions Paul Scofield was pronounced brilliant for his portrayal of Sir Thomas More in his last years as Lord Chancellor of England during the reign of Henry VIII. When Henry failed to obtain from the Pope a divorce from Catherine of Aragon, in order to marry Anne Boleyn, he rebelled by requiring his subjects to sign an Act of Supremacy making him both spiritual and temporal leader of England. More could not in conscience comply. Neither Thomas Cromwell, nor Cardinal Wolsey nor the King himself could get a commitment from him. He resisted anything heroic; he wanted only to maintain his integrity and belief in silence. But this was treason, and his very silence led him to his death. "*'A Man For All Seasons'* is the ageless and inspiring echo of the small voice that calls to us: 'To thine own self be true.' . . . A smashing hit . . . A titantic hit . . . In conception and execution it is a masterpiece."—*N. Y. Journal-American.*

J. B.

By ARCHIBALD MACLEISH

VERSE DRAMA—2 ACTS

12 men, 9 women—Interior

Winner of the Pulitzer Prize for playwriting

The following is from the review of *J. B.* by Brooks Atkinson in the *New York Times:* "Looking around at the wreckage and misery of the modern world, Mr. MacLeish has written a fresh and exalting morality that has great stature. In an inspired performance yesterday evening, it seemed to me one of the memorable works of the century as verse, as drama and as spiritual inquiry. The stage is set . . . in the form of a circus tent . . . Two circus peddlers make whimsical use of the tent by playing God and the Devil. Presently we are deep in the unanswered problems of man's relationship to God in an era of cruel injustices. J. B., a modern business man rich with blessings, is Mr. MacLeish's counterpart of the immortal Job . . . J. B. is brought down by the terrible affliction of our century—deaths and violent catastrophes that seem to have no cause or meaning . . . The glory of Mr. MacLeish's play is that, as in the Book of Job, J. B does not curse God. When he is reunited with his wife, two humbled but valiant people accept the universe, agree to begin life over again, expecting no justice but unswerving in their devotion to God.

Other Publications for Your Interest

AGNES OF GOD

(LITTLE THEATRE—DRAMA)

By JOHN PIELMEIER

3 women—1 set (bare stage)

Doctor Martha Livingstone, a court-appointed psychiatrist, is asked to determine the sanity of a young nun accused of murdering her own baby. Mother Miriam Ruth, the nun's superior, seems bent on protecting Sister Agnes from the doctor, and Livingstone's suspicions are immediately aroused. In searching for solutions to various mysteries (who killed the baby? Who fathered the child?) Livingstone forces all three women, herself included, to face some harsh realities in their own lives, and to re-examine the meaning of faith and the commitment of love. "Riveting, powerful, electrifying new drama . . . three of the most magnificent performances you will see this year on any stage anywhere . . . the dialogue crackles."—Rex Reed, N.Y. Daily News. ". . . outstanding play . . . deals intelligently with questions of religion and psychology."—Mel Gussow, N.Y. Times. ". . . unquestionably blindingly theatrical . . . cleverly executed blood and guts evening in the theatre . . . three sensationally powered performances calculated to wring your withers."—Clive Barnes, N.Y. Post. **(#236)**

COME BACK TO THE 5 & DIME, JIMMY DEAN, JIMMY DEAN

(ADVANCED GROUPS—DRAMA)

By ED GRACZYK

1 man, 8 women—Interior

In a small-town dime store in West Texas, the Disciples of James Dean gather for their twentieth reunion. Now a gaggle of middle-aged women, the Disciples were teenagers when Dean filmed "Giant" two decades ago in nearby Marfa. One of them, an extra in the film, has a child whom she says was conceived by Dean on the "Giant" set; the child is the Jimmy Dean of the title. The ladies' reminiscences mingle with flash-backs to their youth; then the arrival of a stunning and momentarily unrecognized woman sets off a series of confrontations that upset their self-deceptions and expose their well-hidden disappointments. "Full of homespun humor . . . surefire comic gems."—N.Y. Post. "Captures convincingly the atmosphere of the 1950s."—Women's Wear Daily. **(#5147)**

Other Publications for Your Interest

COMING ATTRACTIONS

(ADVANCED GROUPS—COMEDY WITH MUSIC)

By TED TALLY, music by JACK FELDMAN, lyrics by BRUCE SUSSMAN and FELDMAN

5 men, 2 women—Unit Set

Lonnie Wayne Burke has the requisite viciousness to be a media celebrity—but he lacks vision. When we meet him, he is holding only four people hostage in a laundromat. There aren't any cops much less reporters around, because they're across town where some guy is holding *50* hostages. But, a talent agent named Manny sees possibilities in Lonnie Wayne. He devises a criminal persona for him by dressing him in a skeleton costume and sending him door-to-door, murdering people as "The Hallowe'en Killer". He is captured, and becomes an instant celebrity, performing on TV shows. When his fame starts to wane, he crashes the Miss America Pageant disguised as Miss Wyoming to kill Miss America on camera. However, he falls in love with her, and this eventually leads to his downfall. Lonnie ends up in the electric chair, and is fried "live" on prime-time TV as part of a jazzy production number! "Fizzles with pixilated laughter."—Time. "I don't often burst into gales of laughter in the theatre; here, I found myself rocking with guffaws."—New York Mag. "Vastly entertaining."—Newark Star-Ledger.

SORROWS OF STEPHEN

(ADVANCED GROUPS—COMEDY)

By PETER PARNELL

4 men, 5 women—Unit set

Stephen Hurt is a headstrong, impetuous young man—an irrepressible romantic—he's unable not to be in love. One of his models is Goethe's tragic hero, Werther, but as a contemporary New Yorker, he's adaptable. The end of an apparently undying love is followed by the birth of a grand new passion. And as he believes there's a literary precedent for all romantic possibilities justifying his choices—so with enthusiasm bordering on fickleness, he turns from Tolstoy, to Stendhal or Balzac. And Stephen's never discouraged—he can withstand rivers of rejection. (From the N.Y. Times.) And so his affairs—real and tentative—begin when his girl friend leaves him. He makes a romantic stab at a female cab driver, passes an assignation note to an unknown lady at the opera, flirts with an accessible waitress—and then has a tragic-with-comic-overtones, wild affair with his best friend's fiancée. "Breezy and buoyant. A real romantic comedy, sophisticated and sentimental, with an ageless attitude toward the power of positive love."—N.Y. Times.

Other Publications for Your Interest

THE DRESSER

(LITTLE THEATRE—DRAMA)

By RONALD HARWOOD

10 men, 3 women—Complete Interior

Sir, the last of the great, but dying, breed of English actor/managers, is in a very bad way tonight. As his dresser tries valiantly to prepare him to go on stage as King Lear, Sir is having great difficulty remembering who and where he is, let alone Lear's lines. With a Herculean effort on the part of Norman, the dresser, Sir finally does make it on stage, and through the performance—no thanks to the bombs of the *Luftwaffe*, which are falling all around the theatre (the play takes place back stage on an English provincial theatre during an air raid during World War II). It is to be Sir's last performance, though; for backstage in his dressing room after the performance, the worn out old trouper dies—leaving his company—and, in particular, his loyal dresser—alone with their loneliness. "A stirring evening . . . burns with a love of the theater that conquers all . . . perfectly observed, devilishly entertaining backstage lore."—N.Y. Times. "Sheer wonderful theatricality . . . I think you'll love it as much as I did."— N.Y. Daily News. "Enthralling, funny and touching. Lovingly delineated dramatic portraits . . . Almost any actor would jump at them."—N.Y. Post. "A wonderfully affectionate and intelligent play about the theatre."—The Guardian, London.

EQUUS

(Little Theatre-Drama)

By PETER SHAFFER

5 men, 4 women, 6 actors to play horses—Basic setting

Martin Dysart, a psychiatrist, is confronted with Alan Strang, a boy who has blinded six horses. To the owner of the horses the horror is simple: he was unlucky enough to employ 'a loony'. To the boy's parents it is a hideous mystery: Alan had always adored horses, and although Dora Strang may have been a slightly overindulgent mother and Frank Strang a slightly tetchy father, they both loved their son. To Dysart it is a psychological puzzle to be untangled and pain to be alleviated . . . or rather, given his profession, that is what it ought to be. As it turns out, it is something far more complex and disturbing: a confrontation with himself as well as with Alan, in which he comes to an inescapable view of man's need to worship and the distortions forced on that need by "civilized" society. Since this is a story of discovery, the reader's excitement would be diminished by a detailed account of its development. "The closest I have seen a contemporary play come to reanimating the spirit of mystery that makes the stage a place of breathless discovery rather than a classroom for rational demonstration. Mr. Shaffer may have been trying for just such iconography—a portrait of the drives that lead men to crucify themselves—there. Here I think he's found it."—Walter Kerr, N.Y. Times.